MW00879208

A Gangster's BBW Obsession 2

Mz.Lady P

Literary Queen Publications

Contents

Title Page

Table of Contents   2

Chapter 1: Kateevah   3

Chapter 2: Latasia   9

Chapter 3: Draylon   22

Chapter 4: Horse   32

Chapter 5: Kateevah   37

Chapter 6: Belladonna   48

Chapter 7: Keizon   53

Chapter 8: Draylon   58

Chapter 9: Kateevah   68

Chapter 10: Latasia   80

Chapter 11: Horse   90

Chapter 12: Belladonna   99

Chapter 13: Keizon   106

Chapter 14: Kateevah   113

Chapter 15: Draylon   120

The End For Now…   123

MZ. LADY P

Table of Contents

Chapter 1: Kateevah
Chapter 2: Latasia
Chapter 3: Draylon
Chapter 4: Horse
Chapter 5: Kateevah
Chapter 6: Belladonna
Chapter 7: Keizon
Chapter 8: Draylon
Chapter 9: Kateevah
Chapter 10: Latasia
Chapter 11: Horse
Chapter 12: Belladonna
Chapter 13: Keizon
Chapter 14: Kateevah
Chapter 15- Draylon

Chapter 1: Kateevah

It's been months since Draylon and I tied the knot, and life has been nothing short of amazing, rocking his last name. Never in a million years did I ever think we would have such a crazy love story. All I know is that I'm so in love with this man. The way my love has grown for him is unhealthy. I want to live in that man's skin. When we're apart, I feel sad, and when we're together, I'm so happy.

I know I've been driving that man crazy, but I don't care. After finding out the shit that Draylon went through and having fucked up family, I'm definitely all over him. Something inside me makes me want to keep him safe. Like, I know it should be the other way around. Trust me, my man is definitely a protector. After learning how his family was against him, I just felt the need to be overprotective. I hate how obsessed I've become with him. It's supposed to be the other way around.

So far, his mother and grandmother have been going above and beyond to appease him. I lowkey don't trust either of them. Draylon forgave his grandmother because he knew she was influenced by his father and sister. It's as though he and Annalise are the best friends. I've never divulged the secret she told me. Honestly, I never planned to. Draylon really doesn't need to know that part. The bitch was a liar and a deceiver. She deserved death for crossing him like that.

Although, I have my reservations about his mother and grandmother. I'm happy that my daughter loves them. Annalise is currently in rehab and gets to come out on weekends. I'm happy she's sticking to her sobriety. I can tell Horse and Draylon are proud as hell of her. They've been strong about the way things played out with their father and sister. Everything feels so great.

A GANGSTER'S BBW OBSESSION 2

Life is good for everybody. Latasia, my mother, and I are all experiencing the highs of being in love. I can't help but think about how the lows will feel. One thing's for sure, and two for certain, I will do everything I can to be a strong woman for myself and my husband. I love it here, and I'm positive about becoming Mrs. Draylon Prince.

| | | | |

"Latasia, please stop with all the complaining. Your ass is driving everybody crazy." I stressed.

Today was her baby shower, and she had been acting like a real bitch. I felt sorry for Horse. That poor man is catching hell. I bet his ass regrets taking her ass to that stable with his sick ass. That's my bro, though.

"I'm tired. I just want this baby shower to be over." She started crying. All I could do was shake my head. We had spent so much money on this shower, and she had been a bitch all day.

"You need to stop acting like that. My grandbaby's gone come out mean as fuck." Latasia's mom stated as she rubbed on her stomach.

"Leave me alone, La-La!" Tasia pushed past her mom and headed over to where Horse was kicking it with their crew.

"You lucky your ass is pregnant, mean ass heifer!" La-La yelled. Keizon, Latasia, and La-La did nothing but beef with each other.

Somehow La-La managed to get a house out of Keizon, which surprised the fuck out of me, knowing that she ratted him out to the police. Initially, I thought that she wasn't going to do right, but she has been trying her best to be a mother. However, her kids are giving her the hardest time, which is exactly what La-La needs. That's the only way she'll do right. La-La and my mother still hate each other with a passion, but they've found a way to be cordial for the sake of Keizon. They be driving that man crazy with the back and forth.

"Mommy, can I have more cake?" Unique asked.

"No, you've already had two pieces."

"But my daddy said I can have whatever I want because I'm a princess!" she sassed with her hands on her hips. Unique had

4

recently turned seven but acted every bit of seventeen. Draylon had created a spoiled little monster in such a short time. She has really got out of hand.

"I said no! End of story!" I yelled, and she stormed off. I'm pretty sure she was headed to call herself telling Draylon on me, which I didn't care about because I still wasn't giving her anymore cake.

Seconds later, Draylon entered the kitchen. "My baby said you're being mean to her!"

"She wants more cake, Draylon. Her ass only wants sweets. That's why she plays over real food. You and Horse feed her sugar all fucking day. I don't want my daughter growing up fat like me!"

"Why would you say that about yourself? Don't project that onto her. Unique is a child, and children should have sweets. I agree that if she already had a lot, she doesn't need anymore. Just don't be holding her back with thoughts like that. She'll grow up insecure. I don't want my daughter growing up like that."

He walked off before I could say anything. Draylon feels like his word is law. Once he speaks, that's what the fuck it is. The hardest thing is following his lead without being offended. He can sometimes be brutally honest without really realizing he is. Draylon didn't have to say all of that to me. It wasn't necessary.

Observing his grandmother give Unique a piece of cake angered me. I shook it off, though, because I didn't want to kill my mood. However, Draylon was going to hear my mouth. He couldn't keep undermining me in front of her. That's why Unique's ass was getting beside herself. It's cool, though, because I'm about to start whooping her ass. I understand she's crazy about him, and he just wants to make up for lost time. However, I refused to be disrespected in the process.

| | | | |

Later That Night

I was so happy the damn shower was over. Even though I was tired, I was determined to read a little. It had been a minute since I was actually able to sit and read. It's like as soon as I get to reading, I'm interrupted or have to do something. With Draylon and

Unique both sleeping, hopefully, I could get a couple of chapters in.

"Kateevah," he spoke in a low, sleepy tone.

"Yes, Draylon?"

"I love you, baby."

"I love you too."

I closed the book quick as hell and snuggled up under my man. Draylon really pissed me off today, but he never missed a chance to express his love to me. It's that or randomly loving on me every chance he gets. I lowkey think that Draylon knows he went a little too far with his words today. Still, I think it's cute how he genuinely apologizes without physically saying the words. So much for me catching up on some reading. Once I laid my head on his chest, the strong sound of his heartbeat put a bitch right to sleep.

| | | | |

The Next Day

Tired wasn't the word for the way I was feeling. It's a good thing it's Sunday. The shop is closed today and tomorrow, so I'm not doing shit but resting. Tasia wore me out with her pregnancy shenanigans at the baby shower yesterday. I hope and pray her ass doesn't call getting on my nerves today. I love my bestie with everything inside of me, but the bitch is unhinged these days. Hopefully, Horse has the common sense not to get the bitch pregnant again. That man is catching all types of hell from her. Instead of him just giving in and letting her have her way, he matches her energy with his crazy ass. They're so toxic and funny as a couple. At the same time, I can see that they have grown to really love each other. I'm so happy for her. She's about to be a mom and a wife. Lord knows I did think I would see the day that she would ever be either of those things. She deserves a happy life, especially after almost losing hers.

As I handled my personal hygiene, I remembered I hadn't taken my birth control pill. Before Draylon and I decided to make things official, I started taking them. By the grace of God, I hadn't gotten pregnant during that week we spent together, which I was happy as hell about. I didn't want to end up pregnant and be left alone again. I have continued to take them because I'm not ready for another baby right now. My salon is doing numbers, and I want it to stay that way.

As I looked over in the trash can, I observed my pills all emptied out. Without hesitation, I went in search of Draylon. I found him in the office on the phone in a heated conversation. I didn't care, though. He had no right to throw my pills away.

"Why did you throw my pills away?" His eyebrow raised as he narrowed his eyes at me.

"Let me hit you back, Keizon!" He hung up the phone and threw it on his desk. Draylon continued to stare without speaking, and it irritated the fuck out of me.

"Are you going to answer the question or stare at me?"

"Whenever you see me on the phone, you should wait until I'm done before you start speaking! You never know who may be on the other line. Don't ever do that shit again. It's rude as fuck!" he bossed up on me.

I rolled my eyes and walked away. I'm not trying to hear any of that shit Draylon is talking to me right now. Granted, I should have waited until he got off the phone. After all, that is common courtesy. Fuck that shit right about now. I'm angry he did that.

The moment I entered my bedroom, I went into the closet. So much for relaxing. I'm about to go over to my momma's house for a little while. Draylon won't like that 'cause she's back in the city.

"Where are you going?"

"To take Nique to see my momma!" I yelled.

"So, every time we have a disagreement, you go run to your momma's house! That's not how things work. To answer your question, I threw them away because you shouldn't be taking them, anyway. You're my wife! I want a son, Kateevah! What, you don't want to give me more seeds? I thought we were building a family?" he yelled in my face, causing me to damn near jump out of my skin.

"Eventually, I want to have more kids. The salon is doing so well now. Being pregnant will slow me down. Right now, I just want to focus on my business. Please don't take that as me not wanting to give you a son. I swear I'll give you all the babies you want. Just give me a year." I explained as I wrapped my arms around him and stared into his eyes.

"You got it, Mrs. Prince." He kissed me on the lips and left me standing in the walk-in closet.

Now Draylon had me feeling bad. The last thing I want is for him to feel fucked up about not having a baby right now. Instead of me going to the city to see my momma. I decided just to stay home and chill like I initially intended. After all, I had some thinking to do. A bitch needed to figure out if I was going to give my husband what the fuck he wanted.

Chapter 2: Latasia

Being pregnant had been more than I ever bargained for. A bitch was miserable, and I had been making everybody miserable right along with me. Honestly, I feel bad about it. If I'm not crying, my fat ass is eating. I feel like I've gained one hundred pounds. Every time I look in the mirror, I get angrier at Horse 'cause why would he do this to me? To make matters worse, this baby is measuring ten fucking pounds. The man got me carrying a fucking colt around. On the flip side, Horse has been everything he promised and is so attentive to my every need. He is so excited about being a father, which just warms my heart. Honestly, I can't wait to give birth so that I can be nicer to him. Dayvion Prince has been big stepping for a bitch the whole pregnancy. I've fucked around and fell in love with a man that I have a hint of hatred for. It's the most sickening, weirdest thing ever, and I'm sure he be wanting to knock the fuck out of me. The only thing saving me is the baby. I'm positive when I have this baby, that man is going to turn me every which way but loose.

"Hey, daughter."

"Hey, La-La. What are you doing here?" I didn't mean to sound irritated. She just be popping up all of a sudden, acting like the best mother ever. I don't trust it. She's only doing this because we decided to cut her off. I'm shocked that Keizon hasn't pushed her away. Instead, he has allowed her to be around.

"Why is your ass acting so stank with me? Your crybaby ass doesn't be acting ugly when I be rubbing them swole ass hoofs of yours." She came and plopped down on my bed beside me.

All I could do was laugh at La-La. I'm not going to even lie. She has been really supportive. That feels great. However, I can't help but look at her and see dollar signs in her eyes. She knows Horse is rich as fuck.

"You should be rubbing my feet. I'm getting ready to bring your grandchild into the world." I argued.

"I'm so happy about that, Tasia. Look, I came over to talk to you about some serious shit."

"I'm already emotional, La-La. I don't need no bad news."

"It's not bad news. I just wanted to give you this." She reached inside her purse and handed me an envelope filled with money.

"What's this?"

"It's your cut from the house. Some real estate company made me an offer I couldn't refuse."

"What? Really, ma? You love that house."

"Yeah, I do. However, I've been drowning in that house, living off of memories. Your father was everything to me. We never wanted for anything. I never had to do shit but look pretty and be the wife he needed me to be. That's all he wanted. Back then, women followed their husbands. He was worthy of that, and I have no regrets in that department. I would follow Lynwood to the depths of hell if he asked me to. That's how much I loved him. I lived off of your father's love. When he died, I died with him. I've only been here in the physical. All that shit is over with. Going forward, I'm going to be a good mother and great grandmother. I've been depending on you and Keizon instead of it being the other way around. I'm going to do whatever I can to make things right with both of you. From the bottom of my heart, I'm sorry for lying about the mortgage. I promise I'm going to pay you and Keizon back everything."

La-La reached over and hugged me tight around the neck. She had rendered me speechless. I've never seen this side of her. Honestly, it warmed my heart to see her wanting to change.

"I accept your apology, La-La. However, you know it won't be that easy with Keizon. He knows you called the police on him."

"What the fuck are you talking about? I've never called the police on my child! Is that why he's giving me such a hard fucking time?"

"Yes, ma. He says you're the reason he had to do that time."

"Oh, hell nah! I'm to go over to his house. I didn't call no police on him. Keizon's got me fucked up!"

"Ma, don't go over there acting all crazy. The last thing we need is you and Belladonna fighting."

"I'm not about to be tussling with that big bitch. If she tries fighting me again, I'll definitely be the one calling the police. I'm gone get that bitch locked up. No, for real, I really just want to clear the air with him. Look, I love you, and stay off your feet. I'll come by tomorrow and check on you." Before I could say anything, she kissed me on the stomach and rushed out of the room.

Without hesitation, I picked up the phone and sent Keizon a text just to let him know La-La was on the way. That way, he won't be surprised when she pops up.

"Can I get you anything?"

"No, Greta. I'm fine. Thank you for putting all the baby stuff away. It looks so nice."

"Oh, I can't take credit for that. Mr. Prince was adamant about putting everything away. He even packed your hospital bag. Heads up, he's already got the baby coming home outfit together, too. He's so excited. Good night, Latasia."

"Good night, Greta."

I didn't waste any time heading to find Horse. Hearing that made me feel so good. Most men don't even think about doing all of that. As mad as I am about going through this rough ass pregnancy, I'm so happy he's the father of my baby. No matter what happens between Horse and me, I'm sure he'll always take care of our son.

After searching the house, I realized he had left. The nigga didn't even say shit. I decided to sit in his office and order more things I needed from Amazon. As I put things in the cart, email notifications kept coming through. Of course, I had to be nosey and see who was sending him messages. My heart raced, realizing it was from a bitch. I'm not going to even lie. I felt sick as hell looking at the shit. It was a lot of back and forth between them. The fact that Horse had been communicating with this bitch irritated me. I quickly closed the laptop and closed my eyes tight.

Just when I was about to apologize for my behavior, I saw this bullshit.

A pain shot through my back as I headed to my room. I climbed up in bed and tried my best to gather myself. I'm angry and hurt as fuck. I shouldn't even be surprised. We hadn't been able to have sex the way Horse liked. The shit was just too painful. The nigga swore he didn't care about the shit. Of course, he didn't. His ass was still taking bitches to that fucking stable.

I managed to gather myself after hearing his car pull up. There was no way I could address this shit now. It would have to wait until after I gave birth. When Horse walked inside the room, he went into his walk-in closet. He came back out with clothes and a shoebox.

"Where are you going?"

"I'm about to hit Club Bliss for a minute. I have to meet a business associate there."

"Do you have to go at this time of night?"

"Yes, Tasia. I do." He was talking with an attitude, which made me get one.

"Why the fuck are you getting smart?"

"You're the queen of having a smart-ass mouth, so I'm confused as to why you're getting in your feelings."

"I'm not in my feelings. I asked you a fucking question. All of that you're doing is not even necessary, Dayvion!"

I thought he would say something back, but he didn't. Horse walked around the room, getting dressed in silence. The nigga was really mad at me. I wanted to address the situation with him and the bitch but decided not to. My back was hurting all of a sudden. I wanted to tell him, but he might think I was lying so he could stay. Fuck him and that bitch!

Prentiss Women's Hospital

"Don't touch me!" I knocked Horse's hand away from me.

During the night, I went into labor, and he never answered his phone. Business meeting, my ass! I want to kill this motherfucker, but I'm in too much pain.

"You need to stop acting like that, Tasia! Fuck is wrong with you?"

"You nigga! You're what's wrong with me! As a matter of fact, Security! Security! Security!"

"You done lost your motherfucking mind!" The moment Horse approached me, the door opened, and the staff entered.

"Is everything okay?" A security guard asked.

"No! I want him out!"

"Latasia, don't fucking play with me right now!"

"I'm not playing!"

"Come on, sir, you have to leave!"

"Don't put your fucking hands on me, you bitch ass nigga! I'll fuck all y'all up in here, and she knows that!" Horse seethed.

"Just leave, Horse!"

"You got it!" He walked out, and the staff followed behind him.

I pulled the shit up to my eyes and cried like a baby. Deep down inside, I know I'm wrong. It's just hard looking at him, knowing what he has been doing. Seeing that shit made me go into labor, and that's not okay.

The Next Day

The labor pains that I had been going through for the last twenty-four hours were enough for me to get my tubes tied. I swear to God, Horse can never touch me with his big stupid ass dick again. To make matters worse, I have to push out this big-ass baby.

"Mrs. Prince, can I get you anything?" my nurse asked for the hundredth time.

"Yes! Get this fucking demon seed out of me!" I yelled and started crying again.

"Come on now, Latasia! Stop it with all of this. You have to breathe through the pain," my mother urged as she rubbed my back.

"Don't touch me, La-La!"

"That's why your ass is in all that damn pain now! Your ass is mean as hell. I'm going down to smoke a cigarette. I don't have time for this!" she fussed.

I was happy as hell she left.

"Hey, friend. I came as soon as I could." Kateevah rushed in, and I was delighted to see her.

"Thank God! Why won't this baby come?" I burst into tears, and I could see her laughing a little.

"He's going to come. It's just that babies come when they want to, not when we want them to. You need to stop being so mean. Nobody wants to be in here with your ass 'cause you cussing and throwing shit. Why the fuck would you restrict Horse from the room? He's downstairs with his lawyer, you crazy bitch!"

"I was just mad. You'll go tell them I changed my mind. I can't do this without him!"

"Okay. Stop crying. I'll be right back." As soon as Kateevah walked out, my brother walked in.

"Hey, sis. My nephew's giving you hell, huh?"

"Yeah. He won't come out. I've been at five centimeters for the last ten hours. I've been in labor the whole day. I'm not having any more kids. I swear to God, I'm not doing this shit no more. Where the fuck is that doctor? I need drugs!"

"Calm down. That baby is probably not coming because of the way you're acting. You should try calming down."

Before I could respond, Horse walked in. Just looking at his big, tall, long dick ass, I had to fake a contraction to keep from looking at his ass.

"What's up, bro?" Horse spoke.

"Shit. Just ready for my son to be born. You know you're my man one hundred grand. I'm not trying to disrespect you, but your sister got me so fucked up!"

"His sister is right her, and you got me fucked up!"

"Shut up, Tasia! I just told your ass to calm down! You're doing all of this for what?"

"It's cool, Kei. I'm done kissing her ass. Once your sister gives birth to my son, I don't want shit to do with her evil ass. It's straight co-parenting going forth. I don't have to deal with this wishy-washy ass bullshit!"

Before I could respond to what he said, the doctor walked in, along with some nurses. Keizon's phone started ringing, so he rushed out of the room.

"Okay, Ms. Kirkland looks like we're going to have to go ahead with the C-section. They're getting things ready in the OR now. We just need you to sign the paperwork giving us consent to perform the surgery." He handed me a clipboard with some paperwork attached, and I quickly signed it.

"Mr. Prince, here are some scrubs to change into."

"Nah, I don't need them. I'm good. I'll wait out front with the family."

"Are you sure?"

"I'm positive." The whole time Horse talked; he was staring at me. He looked mad as fuck. I was so happy when the nurse left out of the room.

"So, you're going to miss the birth of our son because you're mad at me?" My voice cracked because I was really hurt.

"I don't want to hear none of that shit you are talking about. You've been acting like a mean evil ass bitch! If you weren't pregnant with my fucking son, I would have been beaten your ass. Your mouth is so fucking reckless! You restricted me from the hospital room, so you don't need me in the fucking operating room. My son had just better come into this world one hundred percent okay, or you'll regret it!"

"Are you serious right now?"

"Weren't you serious when you had me restricted? Bitch, I'm no regular ass nigga so stop fucking trying me!"

"Y'all good in here?" Kateevah came inside the room with a look of concern on her face.

"Yeah, we're good." Horse answered and walked out.

I was just stunned and speechless. Yeah, I was wrong for restricting him but damn! Did he have to cuss me out while I was in labor? I'm not saying he shouldn't be mad because I have been acting like a real bitch to him. He could have waited until I gave birth to call me bitches and cuss me out, though.

"Can you please go into the delivery room with me?" I asked

Kateevah as I wiped the tears from my face that had fallen.

"Horse has to be in there."

"Well, he said he's not going in there with me, so please just come in there with me. I'm so scared." I've never felt so scared and weak in my life. I needed to hurry and bring my son into the world so that I could gain my strength back.

"Of course, I'll go in there with you. However, after you heal up bitch, you're gone tell me the real reason you're being mean to Horse. This is bigger than being mad about labor pains. Both of y'all getting on my nerves. I have enough on my plate dealing with Draylon.

Before I could respond to her, the medical staff came in, which I was happy about. Right now, I didn't want to think about Horse. The most important thing was bringing my baby into the world.

| | | | | |

The Next Day

"Oh my god! Look at my beautiful grandson!" Annalise had been marveling at my baby from the moment she entered the room.

I was surprised to see her, seeing as though we'd never formally met. She had been out of state at the Betty Ford Clinic. However, we have spoken on the phone from time to time when she would call Horse.

"He's big, just like his daddy was." Horse's grandmother added.

"Thank you all for coming to see him."

"You don't have to thank us. It feels so good to have grandbabies. For a minute, I thought I would never have grandkids. Where is Horse ass at?"

"He was here earlier, but he left. I'm sure he'll be back soon." I lied. That man hadn't been here since I delivered last night. He spent time with the baby but never said shit to me.

I'm trying to hold it together, but a bitch is torn up inside. I'm mad at myself for bringing Horse's behavior on myself. I'm mad at him for not being able to exercise self-control at a time when I needed him the most. Then again, I just wish I would have been able to put my personal feelings on the back burner.

"Well, I have to get over to the house. If I'm gone too long, Draylon's ass swears I done relapsed. Lord knows I don't want to hear his fucking mouth. Congratulations again, Latasia. Call Granny or me if you need anything." Horse's mother kissed me on the forehead, and his grandmother did the same. It was kind of weird, but I was grateful that they were here loving on my baby.

Once they were gone, I laid the bed back and tried not to think about the pain I was in. A fucking C-section is no joke. I looked over at my ten-pound, thirteen-ounce son and felt complete happiness. Dayvion Jr. was perfect, not to mention worth every tear and every pain. God made him for me, and I plan on being a good mom even if I must co-parent with Horse. No matter what happens between us. I made a promise to be a good mother to my son.

"Where is my god baby?" Kateevah came inside the room with balloons and teddy bears.

"I hope you got some damn food. I'm hungry as fuck! My baby daddy is so mad at me he won't even feed a bitch." I laughed a little, but my feelings are hurt. Horse was really treating me like shit, and I couldn't handle it.

"Of course, I have you something to eat. I stopped by S2 and got you a pot roast dinner."

"Thank you so much." Kateevah placed the food container in front of me, and I wasted no time going in.

"God damn, Tasia! This is a big-ass baby. I see why you been mad and cussing Horse's ass out." She laughed as she took pictures of Junior.

Before I could respond, a text came through my phone. I glanced at the screen and focused back on my food.

Demon Dick: *How is my son doing?*

He wasn't about to get a response from me. If he really cared, he would be here.

"You want me to text him back?"

"Nope. If Horse wants to know, he'll come up here. He's taking his anger out on my baby, and I don't like it."

"This is out of fucking hand, Tasia! What the fuck is going on with y'all? Why in the fuck would you restrict that man from the room in the first place? That shit was dead ass wrong. I would be mad at your ass, too. I'm not saying the way he goes about shit is right. I'm just saying, can you blame him?" Kateevah ranted.

"No matter what I did or why I did it! Horse is wrong for not seeing his son come into the world. That's unacceptable, but I'm not going to dwell on it. I never should have restricted him. He's trying to prove a point to me, and I hear him loud and clear."

"Yeah, but that's still not telling me why you restricted him."

"The night before I went into labor, I was using his laptop to order some things for the baby from Amazon. An email came through with a notification from some bitch named Diwanna Dickerson. She asked him if she could come to 'The Stable'. I went through the messages, and this bitch has been paying him thousands and thousands of dollars to be dominated. Seeing that shit pissed me off so bad."

"Yeah, but he didn't respond to her, so you shouldn't have been mad at him."

"The messages revealed Horse has had sex with her during my pregnancy. Granted, I couldn't let him do the shit to me due to the baby. He just always expressed that he understood. I was so happy and in a comfortable place with him. The moment I saw the messages, all my happiness went away, and I was right back to being mean ass Tasia, who didn't want to be bothered with him. That shit made me go into labor. I'm so hurt, Kateevah!" I pulled my gown up over my face and bawled like a baby.

"Shhhh! It's going to be okay. You went about it all wrong, friend. By you straight restricting him it put you in the wrong. He's looking at you like you're crazy when you have every reason to be mad. I think you need to say something to him. Horse loves you and no one can tell me different."

"I don't question his love for me. I question if I'll ever be enough. That's just one woman, Kateevah! In my heart, I know there is more. I can't even focus right now. I'm supposed to be focused on my beautiful son, not crying my eyes out because his daddy likes to dominate bitches!"

"Shhh! Calm down, Tasia. Listen, try not to think about it right now. I'm sure your ass is in a lot of fucking pain. Getting a C-Section is no joke. Just chill out. Deal with it when you get home and heal up."

"Thank you so much for being here for me. I don't know where I would be without you." I expressed.

Kateevah held my hand through the whole delivery. We cried together, seeing my son for the first time. It broke my heart not to share that moment with Horse. However, I'm glad my best friend in the whole wide world was there to share my experience.

One Week Later

It felt good to finally be home. I was going crazy in that hospital. My blood pressure wouldn't go down, so they wouldn't let me go home. They now have me on blood pressure medication. I can't believe this nigga done gave me high blood pressure, too. This shit is crazy. On a brighter note, I'm so happy my son is a good baby. The only time Junior cries is when his fat ass is hungry. I chose not to breastfeed because it seemed like I wasn't producing enough. Formula has been my best friend. I'm sure Horse has an issue with that because he was adamant about me breastfeeding. I don't care, though.

"Tasia, you need to stop sitting up and holding him like that. He's going to be spoiled." My mother fussed at me as she came and took the baby out of my arms.

"I know, but I just can't stop holding and loving on him."

When I say I'm obsessed with my baby, I am. Junior's so perfect. I've been so foolish calling him a demon seed the whole pregnancy. I wonder if he heard that shit.

Lord, Please show my son that I love him all his days on Earth. I'm sorry for saying all that bad shit while I was pregnant. I was just mad at his daddy. Amen!!

I had to say a silent prayer to God. Hell, I hope he heard me because my mouth was reckless. I'm actually starting to feel so bad about how I've been acting. I never anticipated having the baby and coming home to tension. This is supposed to be a happy time for us. All week, I had time to think about how I wanted to go about things with Horse. I decided to keep shit to myself for the time being. Our son didn't deserve to come home to craziness, so I'm going to wave the white flag. Instead of me acting a fool, I was going to let him hang himself. That bitch in those emails was persistent as fuck. I'm sure we'll cross paths. Mark my words, it won't be pretty.

Honestly, I was glad La-La was going to spend a couple of days with us. That would give me some time to at least work on things with Horse. Surprisingly, he was home today. All week he had been gone to the city on business with Draylon. That's another thing. Lately, they've been in heated ass conversations about business. Apparently, their father and sister owed some fucking Russians. Now, the depth has become a Prince family issue. Horse thinks he be talking low and in codes, but I'm a street bitch, and I know the lingo. Shit is about to get real between them crazy ass Russians and the Prince family. I'm not even worried, though. They got the best hitter on their team. My brother Keizon doesn't miss!

"Can we talk for a minute?" I asked Horse the moment I walked inside of his man cave.

"What do you want to talk about?" he asked but continued to stare at the movie he was watching. Of course, he was about to make it hard for a bitch.

I stood in front of him and blocked his view. He had no choice but to look up at me.

"I just want to apologize for my behavior. Pregnancy was hard on me, and I made it hard for you. That wasn't fair to you. From the bottom of my heart, I'm really sorry, baby."

Horse flamed up a blunt and stared at me with those dark-ass eyes of his. Damn, my baby daddy was fine as shit. No wonder these hoes were paying for it.

"Prove it to me!"

"What?"

"You heard me! You disrespected the fuck out of me! Had you been any other female, I would have murked you for the way you tried to handle me. Then again, I know I'm a lot for a bitch to handle, so the frustration is understandable. However, I'll never play games when it comes to my children. Always know the love I have for my seeds will trump the love I have for you. Make no mistake... that doesn't mean I don't love you or that your crazy ass isn't priceless to me. I just want you to know that I am not that nigga that will allow you to play with my kids. You're smart, so you know exactly what I'm saying. I've never loved a bitch enough to allow her to carry my seed, so consider yourself lucky. You get to be the mother of my children and my wife one day. There is no other woman who will ever have me like you got me, so no matter what you see or come across. Just know there ain't another bitch fucking with you, period! I love you, Latasia. Now come apologize to me, and you better make that shit nasty." He pulled his dick out and started jacking it.

This nigga knew all along why I was acting like that. I could really kill him right about now. However, the positive reassurance got me ready to give him another baby.

"I love you, too. Horse, you know I'm still sore from that C-section."

"And you know my feelings still hurt from being restricted! Come apologize to me. Focus on this dick and not that soreness. You're lucky I can't tie you up and fuck the shit out of you. Now get the fuck over here!"

Horse didn't have to yell twice. I didn't waste time putting my hair up in a high bun. The nigga be skeeting all in my fucking hair and shit. My baby had just laid it all out there for a bitch. I couldn't do shit but focus on the dick. While I was pregnant, I became a pro at giving him head. Just call me a crackhead 'cause these jaws went to work apologizing.

Chapter 3: Draylon

Life knew it could be a motherfucker. A nigga never really knows the sacrifices he must make. The world is filled with snakes and haters. What's fucked up is that you never know who is for you or who is against you. That's why you have to look at everybody around you. You never know where the betrayal will come from.

I've been playing shit cool since I murked my father and my sister. No lie. I cry real nigga tears when I'm by myself. Not for my father but for my sister. Draya was my heart, and I would do anything for her. The fact that she and Shameeka were fucking behind my back really threw me for a loop. Honestly, I would expect that shit from Horse with his freaky ass but never Draya. I'm sure motherfuckers think it was easy for me to cut my father and sister up into pieces. It wasn't. I'll be forever hunted by that image. Murking them has hardened me, and the thirst for blood is overwhelming. Everybody's on my shit list, and anybody can get it.

That's why I'm keeping my mother and grandmother close. I love them ladies, but I'll kill them too if they ever cross me. So far, they've proven to be trustworthy. I'm lowkey happy things have been going in a positive direction with us, but at the same time, I have eyes on them twenty-four-seven.

Horse is the one blood family member who I trust with my life. Dealing with my father and sister's death has been hard as fuck on him, too. We've literally been working ourselves like crazy to keep our minds off the shit. My father was in deep with the Russians. These motherfuckers want ten million from me for a business deal that went south.

Our father negotiated a sale for a commercial property he

thought belonged to our grandfather. Unbeknownst to him, it was a property that had been given to me without anyone's knowledge. Imagine my surprise when these fucking Russians show up thinking it's theirs. Luckily, I found the money they gave him inside a safe in my parents' bedroom. We have a meeting later this week, so I'm going to give them niggas back their bread and be done with the shit. I'm willing to do whatever to keep the peace, but it can definitely be a motherfucking war. Like I said, anybody can get it.

Outside of all the business bullshit, I'm happy to have my wife and my daughter. The day that Kateevah popped up at the crib while I was torturing my people, there I was drenched in blood, and she was holding onto me for dear life. Her not running away spoke volumes. Deep inside of me, I knew I needed to wife her up. Kateevah was riding with me, so I had to give her my last name. That and the fuck that if this shit got out, she wouldn't have to testify against me, which I know she would never do.

Kateevah is loyal as fuck, which is why I hurried up and wifed her. I'm not okay with us getting married at the courthouse. My baby is definitely going to get the wedding she deserves. She and Unique have been the only thing keeping me sane. I really don't think I would have been able to cope had they not been in my life. They make me feel better every day. They love me for me, and that's all I need.

"Good morning, Mrs. Prince," I greeted Kateevah as she cooked breakfast.

"Good morning, daddy," she seductively cooed as she wrapped her arms around my neck.

"Mommyyy, don't call him that! He's my daddy!" Unique was practically about to cry. My daughter was so fucked up about me it was crazy. A nigga loved every minute of it, though.

"Don't be like that. Are you ready for school? Moe will be here in any minute to take you. You look so pretty, daughter." I kneeled in front of her and tied her shoes, followed by placing a kiss on her forehead.

"Yes. Can Uncle Horse come pick me up? I want to go see the baby."

"How about I come pick you up, and we can visit together?" Kateevah suggested.

"Okay, cool. Uncle Moe is here. Bye, daddy, Bye, mommy." Unique grabbed her bookbag and ran out of the kitchen. She didn't even give us a chance to say bye or anything. She loved school, so it was never a problem getting her dressed and out of the door.

My phone started going off, but I ignored it. Right now, I want to spend some time with my wife.

"That could be important. You should answer it." Kateevah placed a plate of food in front of me, and my mouth watered. I realized I hadn't eaten since yesterday.

"What's more important than breakfast with my wife? Come and sit with me. We have an entire staff who gets paid to cook, clean, and be at our beck and call," I reminded her.

"I know that. I'm just so used to doing it. Plus, what type of wife and mother would I be if I let the staff do everything? I'll allow them to do the heavy things. However, I take care of my husband and daughter."

My phone started ringing again, and I ignored it.

"We love you for being a good wife and mother. However, you're like one of those rich housewives now. I just want you to carry yourself like that. It's bad enough you choose to go to work every day."

"Working every day gives me something to do, Draylon. You're never home. I don't want to be here all day by myself. We live more secluded now, so I don't see my momma or Tasia as much. Baby, I'm not complaining because I know why you have us ducked off. It's just that being in this big house gets lonely sometimes. I know you're busy and have a lot on your plate. You don't need me being a nagging woman because you're never home. It's good that I have something to do while you're out working. Trust me, I'm not mad about the long hours. You're the boss, baby, and I am aware of what I signed up for." Kateevah leaned across the table and kissed me.

"Thank you for understanding and being patient. I know

you're still getting used to living life with me. I promise you things will get better."

"Since we're talking about things getting better. I decided not to take the pills anymore. You're my husband. If you want a baby, then a baby you shall you get."

"I want a son, Kateevah."

"I know that, but if I get pregnant. There is a possibility I'll have a girl." She was laughing, but I was dead ass serious.

"I want a son, end of discussion. Thank you for deciding not to take the pills and for breakfast. I love you, Kateevah."

"I love you, too." We kissed, and she quickly left the table. I'm sure she was in her feelings about my stance. A namesake is what I want. I already have a daughter. All I need is my Junior to make things complete.

My phone started going off again, and it was from my granny. Instead of answering, I sat eating the rest of my breakfast. Today is Monday, and we always have morning meetings, so I'm sure she's calling to see why I'm late. Hopefully, she has all the paperwork signed that I need to fully take over all the real estate she owns. She had been letting my father run the properties, which was bad all the way around because he hadn't taken care of them. Numerous buildings were on the verge of financial collapse, all because he had been pocketing everything. The motherfucker was a snake to his mother, too.

| | | | |

The Prince Estate

"I'm sorry. I'm late, Granny," I apologized as I kissed her on the forehead, then dapped it up with Horse.

"It's okay. Horse just walked his ass in here, too. Have a seat. Let's get this meeting over with. I have to take Unique her lunch."

"Kateevah fixed Unique's lunch this morning."

"Yeah, but she only gives her half of a turkey sandwich, apple slices, and a bottle of water. The girl is in second grade. She needs a fun lunch. I know Kateevah is trying to keep her weight under control. However, I think she's a little overboard with it. My Granny Girl's been texting me every day asking me to bring her lunch."

"Unique got all of us working for her. She had me bring her a Happy Meal last week," Horse added.

I couldn't do shit but laugh. My daughter was sneaky as fuck.

"I'm going to speak to Kateevah about that. Let's get down to the business at hand."

I needed to quickly change the subject. Lately, Kateevah had been doing some real insecure shit that I didn't like. My wife had no reason to feel anything but comfortable around me. That shit got me so fucking heated.

"Here are all the documents with the properties and the deeds. You and Horse can split it up as you see fit. I'll handle everything with my name on it. Also, I'm stepping down, and you now have my seat on the board. You and Horse now have total control over all things Prince."

"Why are you giving it all up now?" I inquired. It was imperative I knew. Just a minute ago, she basically snatched the shit from me.

"Because it's rightfully yours. That and the fact that I promised your grandfather everything would eventually be turned over to you, not to mention I made such a bad judgment call with your father and sister. Let me know when it's time for me to step down. I was supposed to see that things weren't right, yet my love and loyalty to my son trumped common sense. Draylon, I am sorry for everything that happened. I'm sorry to you, too, Dayvion. I should have trusted your judgment."

"I accept your apology, granny. You already know that. With you stepping down, what are you going to do to stay busy?" Horse asked.

I was listening to them but was also busy going through the paperwork.

"I'm going to relax and be a real grandmother for a change. My great grandkids need me. I've put my work in and kept my promise to your grandfather. It's y'all turn to take the Prince family to whatever level you see fit. You have my blessings." Granny stood up from behind her desk and embraced me and Horse. I knew she was being real with handing everything over.

"Do you have any advice you want to give us before you've officially stepped down?" I inquired.

"You need to kill Nikolav and the entire Evanoff family. Annihilate them, and you become the chairman of the board, which gives the Prince family complete and total reign of the city. Nikolav has held that seat because neither your grandfather nor father didn't have the balls to eliminate his father or grandfather. But you two, you're absolutely built for it. Make your grandmother proud.

"Say less." I laughed, watching her and Horse dap it up. They were always so close.

"Now we have to come up with another plan," Horse stated as we walked out of the house.

"No, we don't. We're going to stick to the plan. They're under the impression that we're coming to give them the bread, so that's how it will appear. We're just gone add a little razzle-dazzle if you know what I mean, lil' bro."

"So, you are bringing out the big guns, huh?"

"Hell yeah, that's the only way we're going to annihilate them motherfuckers. Let's head over to the office to go over this paperwork."

"I'll meet you there. I have to run to the bank and check out the safety deposit boxes pops left behind."

"You need me to roll with you?"

"Nah, I'll call you if I find some interesting shit."

"Okay. Hit me later."

Hopping in my car, I headed to our headquarters, contemplating the future. The chairman of the board position was a tenured seat, so you can't be voted out. The only way you lose your position is if you die. Yeah, this shit is about to get way too real for the Prince family.

Later That Night

All day, I had been anticipating getting home to talk to Kateevah. She had been on my mind all day to the point where I couldn't focus. It was late, but I was hoping she was still awake. There was no way I could sleep without having a conversation with her. I blew up at her in the kitchen for denying our daughter more cake. I'm sure she thinks it was me undermining her, but it wasn't. I went against her because I knew she was denying our daughter due to weight. That's not how I want either of them to live.

Before heading into our bedroom, I checked on Unique. She had fallen asleep playing on her iPad. I shut it off and placed a kiss on her forehead. When I entered our bedroom, Kateevah was sitting in bed reading a book.

"Get up!"

"Huh?"

"I said get up, right now!" She quickly put the book down and jumped out of bed.

"What's going on?" I yanked her hard as fuck and made her stand in front of the floor-length mirror.

"Look in that fucking mirror and tell me what you see!" I demanded.

"I-I don't know. I-I see us." She stammered over her words.

"You know what I see? I see a woman with the world at her feet but is too insecure to enjoy it."

"What are you talking about, Draylon?" Kateevah sounded shocked and offended.

"Let me help you out. What I see is the most beautiful woman in the world. Your weight is by far the sexiest thing on you. Don't you know that's what I love most about you? You're so pretty, Kateevah. My dick gets hard just looking at them pretty ass feet. I'm not sure the woman you were before I came into your life. However, I'm in your life now, so all this lowkey insecure bullshit has to stop. When you step into any room, you better own that motherfucker because you do. What, you don't think you're good enough for me or something?"

"I know that I'm good enough for you, without a motherfucking doubt. As far as me being insecure. I'm not insecure about us in the way that you think. I'm very comfortable with my body, Draylon. I also know that you love all of me. That's why I love you with everything inside of me. I'm insecure about us as a couple. Every day, when I wake up, I get on my knees and pray for our family. I'm scared and insecure that I'll lose you. Every day, when you leave, I be thinking you're not coming back." She sounded like she was about to cry, so I quickly wrapped my arms around her.

"Stop crying, baby. I'm going to always come home to you. God didn't bring us back together for him to just snatch it all away. This thing we have is just beginning. The best is yet to come. Stop worrying and enjoy our life together. When I walk out that door, it's imperative that your mind is filled with nothing but positive energy. Any negative thoughts will bring forth negative energy. We don't need anything negative in our lives. Life is so fucking good right now. Don't you agree?" I grabbed some Kleenex and wiped the tears from her face.

"Yes."

"Are you happy, Kateevah?"

"Yes! Baby, you make me so happy. I'm just scared to lose you." She fell into my arms and started crying hysterically.

"Shhh! Stop crying." I gently pushed her back onto the bed and parted her legs. Eating her pussy was probably the only thing at the moment that would calm her down.

"Baby, what are you doing?" she asked as I pulled her panties down. Kateevah was squirming all around like a fish out of water.

"I'm about to eat your pussy. Do you think that would make you feel a little better?" Before she could answer, I started feasting on her pussy.

"Oh my god! Yes, baby! You're making me feel so good."

"I'm...going...to...always...come... home... to... you."

I placed a kiss on her clit with each word that I spoke. A nigga meant each and every motherfucking word. I'll always come home to my family because I'm never going to let some fuck nigga gun me down. I'm *that nigga* who puts niggas' mothers and bitches on that front pew! Kateevah and Unique will never experience seeing me like that. I'm that gangster that's going to grow old and see the

Prince family take over the motherfucking world.

| | | | |

Hours Later

"I'm sorry for having a meltdown," Kateevah apologized as we passed a blunt back and forth. We had just finished making love and were just up chilling with one another. I was happy as fuck she had calmed down.

"It's okay. Baby, you expressed your feelings, which is something I want you to do. Don't ever be afraid to speak your mind. I love you."

"I love you, too. Damn, the sun is getting ready to come up. Let me get up and cook breakfast. I need to pack Unique's lunch and get her clothes ready."

"Baby, don't get offended when I say this, but Unique hates the lunch you make her."

"Why do you say that? Her lunch box be empty every day, and she be telling me she ate it all."

"Our daughter has been calling Granny and Horse to bring her food for lunch every day. I understand that you're concerned about Unique's weight but she's a kid baby. It's okay to send her with healthy shit but send her some good shit too. We do everything in moderation, anyway. She'll be okay, Kateevah. You be acting like she's obese, and she's not."

"I just don't want Unique to be fat. I'm just afraid that she will get teased and bullied. Kids can be so cruel. When I was her age, I was teased about my weight, so I can see how I've been projecting that insecurity onto her. I'll do better with her lunches. I'm also going to call Granny and Horse and tell them not to be taking her restaurant food, either."

"Good luck with that. You know Unique has them wrapped around her finger."

"I know, right. Let me get up and get breakfast ready." She kissed me on the cheek and climbed out of bed.

I marveled at her naked body as she walked into the master bedroom. My wife was the baddest BBW walking, and she had no clue. I'm going to make it my business to pipe my wife the fuck up.

Kateevah Prince is the coldest in the city, and I want the world to know that.

Chapter 4: Horse

Being a father had given me a new sense of purpose. I've never really cared about much, but my son, Dayvion Jr., made me soft as fuck. He's the only reason I haven't killed Latasia's crazy ass. Plus, I done fucked around and fell in love with the bitch. I've never felt like I was in over my head with some shit. However, Latasia was a fucking handful. At the same time, I can't see myself being with any other woman. I trust her, and I know she's loyal to me.

That's why I hated she saw those emails from Diwanna. She's a female I've been dominating for years. Our fathers were in business together. When I was sixteen, I accompanied my father out to Miami for a business meeting he had at their crib. While he handled business, I was left to entertain Diwanna. I broke her out of her virginity that day. We've never been official or in a relationship. It's just that every time she comes to the Chi for business, she hits me up for the dick, but she has to pay for it every time.

I never saw Diwanna being any more than just somebody to fuck. Any bitch that loves a nigga so much she'll pay for the dick is insane. At the same time, we've always been cool and honestly only friends, giving each other advice and shit. Diwanna is smart as fuck. She's good at investments, stocks, and bonds. Shit like that. The bitch knows about numbers, not to mention the fact that she's monied the fuck up. The bitch is a billionaire, so she has to pay for this dick every time.

Shit has changed, though. Her money is nothing to me. I want shit to work with Latasia. I'm a family man now, so I can't be dominating bitches anymore. I admit I have fucked with a bitch or two since we became official. However, I'm ready to just create the life I want with my nutty-ass baby momma. She is so fucking beautiful. My son got her thick than a motherfucker. Every time she's in my presence I have to refrain from tying her up and fucking her.

As I sit watching her get dressed for our date. My dick is getting hard. That pussy is ready for a nigga now. I'm about to get her drunk and fuck the shit out of her. I have not forgotten how she handled me, so that pussy is getting punished.

"Stop looking at me like that, Horse!"

"What! I can't look at you?" I laughed as I took a long pull from my blunt.

"You got that wild look in your eyes. You can't wait to fuck me in that stable," she called me out.

"It's a good thing you know. Stop acting like you don't want me to fuck the shit out of you." I smacked her hard as hell on the ass, followed by engaging in a passionate kiss.

"Y'all going out or what?" La-La asked, peeking her head into our bedroom.

"Yes, ma! We're leaving now. Hey, Fat Daddy! Momma's gone be right back, okay? Are you sure we can't take him with us, Horse? Look at him. He's sad. My baby knows we're about to leave him."

"No. He can't go with us, babe. I'm going to miss him, too. We need a night out. Let's go!" I had to practically yank her out of the room. I'm crazy as fuck about my son, but Latasia is obsessed with him.

The moment we got inside our waiting car. I could tell her nutty ass was about to cry. All I could do was laugh.

"Nothing is funny, Horse. I've never been away from him since he was born. I feel scared. You think La-La gone be able to handle him?"

"If I didn't think La-La could do it, she wouldn't even be in our crib. She's good with him and will take good care of him. Stop worrying. It's all about me and you tonight. You got panties on underneath that skirt."

"Nope."

"Spread your legs so I can play in that pussy." I didn't even give her a chance to say anything as I roughly opened her legs and found my target.

| | | | |

K1 Seafood & Co.

"This food is so fucking good! How come I never heard of this place?"

"They just opened. This is one of my associate's restaurants. As a matter of fact, here the nigga goes now." I wiped my mouth and got up to greet my nigga KJ.

"My nigga Horse. Thanks for coming by and fucking with us. You already know this shit is on the house!"

"Nah, nigga you know I'm paying that bill, especially since you've been fucking with the Prince family for a minute. This is my future wife, Latasia."

"What's up? Congratulations on the baby."

"Thank you. Where is the bathroom?"

"Straight to the back. Aye, Yah-Yah, show her the bathroom!"

"Nigga, do I look like a motherfucking tour guide! Come on, boo!"

I laughed because each and every time I saw KJ's sister, she was with the shits. I'm glad Latasia laughed it off. We don't need bullshit today.

"Have you thought any more about that Rico situation?" KJ inquired.

"Nah, I'm not really feeling having a sit-down with his people. That nigga is dead, and I'm the one who murked them. Fuck they want to talk about with me?" Rico's crew has been talking all types of shit in the streets. Threats have been sent my way and all. These motherfuckers don't know I take threats very seriously.

"I understand that. With Draylon trying to get that seat on The Roundtable, it's imperative the beef is squashed. You already know that was bitch move Rico pulled, so he had to be dealt with. Honestly, I think they want his body or some shit."

"Well, them bitch ass niggas still wasting their fucking time. There ain't no piece of that motherfucker that still exists. I'll talk with my big bro, and I'll get back with you in regard to that sit-down."

"Say less."

KJ and dapped it up just in time. Tasia was headed back to the table, and she had no clue the Rico situation might just be a problem. Trust me. It's not a problem that can't be handled accordingly. I just don't want my baby even stressing about that nigga. Every time I see the bullet wound on her chest, I become irate on the inside. Them motherfuckers had better hope I don't agree to the sit-down. Just to kill all of them motherfuckers for what the fuck he had done to her and Kateevah.

"Come on, baby. Let's get out of here. There's a stable calling your name."

"We got to stop and get some Julio first." I laughed because this woman insisted on getting tipsy before letting me beat the pussy up. I dropped a couple of one-hundred-dollar bills on the table.

We headed out of the restaurant at the same time that a female I fucked with from time to time was coming in with her crew. I could tell by the looks on Kimmie's face she was about to pull a stunt. She was a stripper bitch I met at Club Bliss. It was nothing serious at all. Just a fuck here and there. Still, the bitch was about to put a ten on two.

"Damn, just a minute ago, you were fucking my brains out. Now you ain't gone speak?"

"And he's not! Beat it, bitch!" Latasia quickly stepped in Kimmie's face.

"I'm not talking to you!"

"And my man is not speaking to you! Let's go, Dayvion!" Latasia snatched me hard as fuck in my collar like I was her son or something. I could hear Kimmie and her wack-ass crew talking shit in the distance. That hoe had better hope I don't see her ass again and slap slob from her mouth.

"Let me go before you stretch my fucking Gucci polo out!"

"You had better get these hoes in check!" Before I knew it, she had slapped the fuck out of me.

"Why the fuck would you do that, Latasia?"

"'Cause you need to get your bitches in order! I will not be played with! I'm going to smack your ass every time I feel disrespected!"

"If I smack you back you gone say I was wrong. Look, that's a bitch I fucked a time or three. Nothing serious. She was just in her feelings because she saw me with you. Fuck that hoe! Don't let that bitch ruin our night!"

"I'm not about to let her ruin our night. However, you're going to ruin the rest of your life if you don't get these hoes under control. I swear to God I'm going to kill your ass, Horse! Let's get to the damn liquor store. I need a drink. I swear you make me hate your ass sometimes."

"You say it's hate, but I know you love a nigga. Look at my dick. You got my dick hard as fuck, right now. My baby is all jealous and shit over me. You got a real nigga blushing and shit!"

"Shut up, Horse! I'm not jealous, period!

"You better be! Shit, every time a hoe steps to me in your presence, you better check that bitch. I'm never going to let a bitch cross a line with you, but at the same time, you better let them hoes know you my bitch."

I grabbed Tasia by the face roughly and shoved my tongue down her throat. No matter how I handled a bitch. When a hoe steps wrong, she better make that bitch step right.

Chapter 5: Kateevah

I had been running around like crazy getting things together for Annalise. She had successfully completed rehab, so Draylon wanted to give her a big party. In all honesty, she deserved it. Annalise had worked hard to gain her sobriety. I'm also proud of her, so helping Draylon pull this party off was no problem. We would be meeting some more of their relatives. I was cool with that because it meant Unique would meet more of her family.

"Do you need help?" my mother asked as she came into the kitchen.

"Nah, I'm good, ma. You look cute."

"Girl, Keizon is talking shit. Talking about my titties all out."

"Because they are! Gone make me nut the fuck up!" he interjected before grabbing a beer from the fridge and walking out.

My momma and I fell out laughing.

"That man swears niggas be at me. Little does he know they won't even step to me because I'm his wife. Keizon is so damn jealous. He was never this way before we got married."

"Oh please, ma! You love to make that man act crazy."

"And do!"

"What are y'all in here laughing about?" Tasia asked as she came into the kitchen and took a seat across from me.

"At Keizon's crazy ass. He's mad cause he says my titties are out. They're big as fuck, so any damn shirt I have on, they're going to be out."

"I mean, you do look like you gone put somebody damn eye out with those things." Tasia joked, causing all of us to laugh.

"Fuck you! I'm about to go up to your room and find another shirt. If I don't, he's going to try holding out on the dick, and a bitch can't have that now."

I just shook my head at her as she walked away. My momma and Keizon were a whole mess of a couple. They're so obsessed with each other, and I think it's cute. I've never seen her so happy. Keizon keeps my momma with a smile on her face. Growing up, I've always seen her fuck with niggas, but none of them truly cared for her. I'm happy it's Keizon. His love for her is genuine. I can also tell how much my momma loves him and motivates him. That nigga has been a homebody since he tied the knot. Draylon and Horse have to basically drag him out of the house. He wants to live in Belladonna's skin.

"What's up, best friend?" I asked Tasia.

"I'm a little tired. Your godson was up all night, so I didn't get much sleep. The one night that La-La decides to go home, his ass would stay up. I swear I wanted to whoop his fat butt."

"Bitch, you better not touch my baby. Let's take some shots. I'm done with everything I had to prepare for the party. The caterers are going to do the rest."

"Good. I definitely need a shot or something." I watched her as she winced in her seat.

"You good?"

"My ass is just a little sore from Horse spanking me." She laughed and blushed at the same time.

"That nigga done turned you the fuck out." The shit Tasia be telling me about that damn stable is crazy.

"Don't judge my man! Punishing this pussy is his love language."

"Yeah, okay. Keep it up. Your ass is going to be walking pregnant again. I'm telling you right now I'm not dealing with y'all shit again." Latasia and Horse do not need to have any more kids. They both drove the whole family crazy.

"I got that damn Depo shot. I'm not trying to have another baby anytime soon."

I poured both of us some shots, and we knocked them back. My phone started going off, and I quickly ignored it. My father had been trying to reach out to me, but I just wasn't feeling. All of my life, he has been an inconsistent presence, so I'm just not in the mood to deal with him at the moment.

"Who was that?"

"My daddy. You know he comes around twice a year, swearing he wants to spend more time with me. The last time we spoke, he promised Unique he would take her to Navy Pier. He had me get her dressed, and he never showed. I don't care about him not showing up for me. When he doesn't show up for her, shit changes."

"I feel you on that. I've been skeptical about La-La, too. So far so good, though. I'm actually happy that she's stepping up to be a good grandmother. Lord knows she hasn't been a good mother in a long time."

"The good thing is that she's making an effort. I really love that for you and Keizon. Off topic. Outside of everything that has happened, are you happy, friend?'" I poured both of us another shot and waited for her to respond.

"Yes, I am. Honestly, I never imagined that I would be living so good. Every morning, I roll over to Horse snoring loud as fuck, and realize he has made me so happy. No matter how much I talk shit or fuss at him, I love that man, friend. Thank you for having that one-night stand. Because of that, I'm a mother and getting ready to be Mrs. Dayvion Prince."

"You're already Mrs. Dayvion Prince!" Horse confidently spoke as he walked into the kitchen. I smiled, watching him and Tasia love on each other.

"Y'all need to get a room."

"Good idea. Come here, let me talk to you for a minute." Tasia seductively purred and grabbed him by the hand.

"I don't care what room you freaky motherfuckers go in. It just better not be my room." Tasia be talking all that shit about Horse and that demon dick. Her ass done got addicted to that shit. Just a minute ago, she was wincing. Now she was walking like ain't shit wrong with her.

"Mommyyyy!" Hearing Unique calling me made me rush out to the living room.

"Daughterrr!" We laughed, and I kissed her on the forehead. Draylon, Granny, and Annalise had all come inside the house.

"Look at my beautiful daughter-in-law." Annalise rushed over and wrapped her arms around me.

"Hey, Annalise. I'm so proud of you." I made sure to embrace her tightly. From the moment we met that crazy ass day, she has been so sweet and accepting of me. I'm not sure if it's because I know her secret or if it's because she truly fucks with me. Either way. It feels good not to have a monster in law fucking with me.

"Thank you. One day at a time. I couldn't have done this without my boys, you, and Granny."

"What about me, grandma?"

"I'm sorry, grandbaby. I couldn't have done it without you, either."

"What's up, baby? I missed you." Draylon spoke as he wrapped my arms around my waist.

"I missed you too. Everything is set up for the party. I've paid all the vendors already. All you have to do is celebrate with your mom."

"Thanks, baby. I appreciate it. I'm going to go change. I'll be back down shortly." He kissed me on the lips and headed up the stairs. At the same time, the doorbell started ringing.

Before I could answer it, Annalise stopped me.

"I'll get it, Kateevah. It's more than likely my brothers."

"Oh, lord! Let me get a drink. Come on, Unique. Let's get us some cocktails." Granny didn't hesitate to get up and leave.

"I want a virgin strawberry daiquiri!" she requested. "I always be drunk off those."

My daughter really thought that she be getting drunk with Granny. It was the funniest shit to watch. Granny has her believing that they have liquor in it. Unique is crazy about her Uncle Horse, but she loves her some Granny. They call themselves besties. As much as I love the fact that my baby has her family, I hate that they are bad influences on her. It's mind-boggling to see that they don't think that they are. Still, I just have to let them do them. No one with the last name Prince listens to anyone.

I focused on the door and observed a female step inside the house. Without hesitation, I sized her up. She was statuesque and snatched to perfection.

"What the hell are you doing here, Nautica?"

"Hello to you too, Mrs. Prince. I've been out for about a week. Draya hasn't been answering the phone for me. I got this address from Granny."

Hearing that angered me. *Why the fuck would she give our address out?*

"Nautica!" I turned to see Draylon walking toward us.

"Draylonnnnnnn!" the chick screamed and jumped on him. Seeing her kiss him on the lips let me know she was more than just a friend.

"Whoa! You can't be doing that shit, Nautica! My wife is standing right here." It seemed as though all the color drained from her face. Her entire demeanor had quickly changed. She quickly took a step back.

"Nautica!" Horse spoke as he and Tasia came into the living room.

"Heyyy, Horse. I missed you, brother."

"Aht-aht! Not too much on my man!" Tasia quickly stepped in between them.

"Where is Draya? This is too much going on." The bitch dramatically threw her long hair over her shoulder.

"Draya is dead. Come with me, Nautica." Annalise stated while grabbing her hand.

The moment they were out of the room. Draylon walked over to me, but I stepped back. The sight of that bitch lip gloss on his lips angered the fuck out of me.

"Kateevah!"

"No. Don't talk to me until you wipe your fucking lips!" I fumed.

I tried walking away, but he yanked me back.

"Don't walk away from me. Let me talk to you." He grabbed my hand, and we headed up the stairs. I was so mad with jealousy that I was shaking. With each step, I tried calming down. I wasn't used to other women around him. Shameeka was different. She was his wife before we made things official. However, now, Draylon is mine, and I don't want him close to no bitch. I don't care who it is.

The moment we entered our bedroom, Draylon closed the door behind us. He walked into our bathroom and came back out with a towel, wiping his mouth. His ass better had wiped that bitch off him because there was no way I was saying a word had he not done so.

"Who the fuck is she, Draylon?" I didn't hesitate to get to the matter at hand the moment he sat next to me on the bed.

"That's Nautica. She and Draya were best friends."

"Then why was she kissing on you like you were her nigga or something?"

"Because when she went away eight years ago, we were a thing. She was a foster kid, and my parents took her in. Honestly, she's like a sister, too."

"That bitch isn't your sister no more! The two of y'all used to fuck, so I'm not trying to hear no sister bullshit. Draya's dead, and she will be, too, if she thinks about playing with me. That little kiss downstairs better be the only encounter you two have. I'm telling you now, if I even think some slick shit is going on, I'm going to nut the fuck up." I warned.

"You don't play about me, huh?" Draylon laughed and pulled me on his lap.

"I won't ever play about you, especially when it comes down to another woman. What's that they be saying? This shit is until the casket drops. I mean that. I'll kill you, her, and any other bitch who tries to destroy my family. It's you, me, Unique, and all the future babies we're going to have! There is no room for no motherfucking body else! Come on. Let's go celebrate Annalise."

I kissed him on the lips and left his ass sitting there thinking, which is exactly what I wanted him to do. Draylon lowkey thinks I'm weak and insecure, which doesn't feel good. I'm neither of those things, but I am jealous when it comes to him. I'll never be apologetic about that, and I don't care what anyone thinks.

"I don't trust that bitch, friend!" Tasia stated.

"If the bitch was Draya's best friend, that hoe definitely can't be trusted. To make matters worse, she and Draylon used to fuck around, so you know I don't want that bitch around at all."

We were in the kitchen staring out of the window into the backyard. Horse, Granny, and Annalise were all talking to the bitch, which irritated me. Seeing her bend down to speak to my daughter angered the fuck out of me. However, I held my composure because this bitch wasn't about to see me act out of character.

"I hope Horse knows I'm gone slap the fuck out of him." Tasia ranted.

"Why? What did he do?"

"I don't like how she's all over him. If you ask me, she probably fucked him and Draylon."

"The bitch fucked Draya too! Best friend, my ass! Knowing that she fucked Shameeka, I don't put shit past her. I'm not trusting the fact that she just came out of the fucking blue and popped up. Granny giving her this address really got me looking at her sideways. She could have had that bitch come to her house, not the fucking house he shares with his wife and daughter. That's out of line, not to mention strike one against her old ass. Annalise has a strike against her, too. I'm not feeling them being out there with that bitch like it's a family reunion. I'll kill all they asses about my respect!"

"And you're not wrong! Trust and believe I'm right with you. Let's go out here and get fucked up. If she even blinks wrong, we're gone beat her ass."

"Both of y'all need to cut it out!" Draylon spoke, interrupting us, but I waved his ass off.

Tasia and I laughed hard as hell at him. I looked back and could tell he didn't like that, but so what. There will be no more lacking when it comes to threats against this family, especially when it's the family that hurts you. I couldn't care less about her being adopted. All of that shit went out of the window the moment she fucked him. Talking about she's like a sister... sister, my ass. I'm not respecting that bitch at all, so Draylon can stop thinking I'm going to be accepting her.

| | | | |

Uniquely Yours Nail Bar

Owning a nail bar was never something I aspired to do. Hair has always been my thing. Draylon had an empty storefront and basically gave it to me. He told me to do whatever I wanted, so I made it a nail bar. I don't do nails, so I hired some of the dopest Black nail techs I could find. It made me so damn happy to see every chair with a client. With this being the grand opening, I couldn't ask for a better turnout.

"Congratulations, baby girl."

Looking up from the front desk, I locked eyes with my father, Kato. He had an enormous bouquet of roses. I hadn't spoken to him, so I was surprised to see him here. I wanted to ask what he was doing here. Instead, I embraced him. Honestly, it felt good to see him.

"Thank you, daddy."

"I know you've been kind of pissed with your pops. For that, I'm sorry. I have never been there for you like I should. Just know I'm going to go above and beyond to make it up to you."

"Don't worry about making anything up to me. Let's just focus on rebuilding our relationship. I'm an adult now, so I don't harbor any ill feelings toward you. However, we will fall out when it comes to Unique. Don't ever tell her you'll spend time with her and don't show up. You hurt her feelings, daddy. She waited for you to come that day, so you owe your granddaughter an apology. I'll never allow you to disappoint her the way you have done me. I love you, daddy. Thanks for coming to my grand opening. It means a lot to me." I asserted.

It was as if a weight was lifted off of my shoulders. I had finally found the courage to speak my mind to my father. He needed to know how I felt. As we embraced once more, I looked up to see my mother. The look on her face let me know she was irritated seeing Kato.

"Damn! Look at you, Belladonna! Damn, girl, you look good as fuck!" My father quickly rushed over and lifted my mother off of the ground, followed by kissing her on the lips. She quickly jumped down.

Keizon and Draylon had walked into the shop right at that moment. The look on Keizon's face let me know he was pissed.

"This is Kateevah's father, Kato. Kato, this is my husband, Keizon." she introduced.

"You're married?" my father questioned with a surprised look on his face. I'm sure it was because he didn't know she was married, not to mention to a younger nigga.

"Daddy, this is my husband and Unique's father, Draylon. Draylon, this is my father, Kato." I introduced.

"It's nice to finally meet the man who fathered my granddaughter. For a minute, I thought you didn't exist."

My eyes bulged out of my head at hearing my father say that. Honestly, it angered me. He didn't have a right to say that.

"Nah, I'm one hundred percent real. I'm Draylon Prince, but you know that already. Ain't that right, Kato? I'll see you at the crib, Mrs. Prince." Draylon kissed me and walked back out of the shop.

Confusion was the only word I could think of. The look on my father's face was confusing, too.

"I'll talk to you later." Keizon gritted and walked away. He was pissed the fuck off.

"What the hell you want, Kato? I'm telling you now, don't for a second think you're about to come around and fuck up our lives. For the first time in forever, we have truly found happiness. Do us a favor. Don't be on no bullshit. Be a father and grandfather!"

"I'm not on no bullshit, Belladonna! How the fuck was I supposed to know your young nigga was jealous? Since when you started picking up niggas at the playground, anyway?" Kato defended.

Before I could do anything, my mother reached back and slapped the fuck out of my daddy. The entire shop ceased hearing that smack.

"Ma!"

"Nah, It's cool, baby girl. I just came to see you and tell you congratulations. I love you and my grandbaby. I'll be in touch." My father kissed me on the cheek and proceeded to leave.

"That's right, motherfucker! Get the fuck on! Do what you do best, you fucking deadbeat! Does your wife know you're here? I bet she doesn't! Take your ass back where you been, bringing your ass around stirring up bullshit! I hate your ass, nigga!" my mother yelled and started launching fingernail polish at him.

Kato was trying his best to duck and dodge them, but Belladonna kept launching them bitches at him. So much for a successful grand opening.

Looking around, I could see the customers with their phones recording. This shit was definitely about to go viral. I felt sorry for my dad a little. I'm sure he didn't come with the intention of pissing off my mother. One thing I know is that he loves him some Belladonna. He was jealous, learning that my mother had got married, which confused the fuck out of me because he was a married man. That's a nigga for you, though. They don't want you, yet they don't want anyone else to have you.

"I'm so sorry, Kateevah. I ruined your grand opening. I'll replace everything and get this cleaned up." Belladonna voiced.

"No, ma! You didn't. It was a success. Come on. Let's go have a drink and celebrate. Hey Shani, can you clean this up for me and run things for a little while?"

"I got you, Kateevah." My assistant, Shani, quickly started getting the polish up.

"I'll call you later. Let me get home. Keizon is about to go off on me."

"But you didn't do anything."

"We know that. However, he walked in to see Kato hugging and kissing on me. Keizon is feeling disrespected by me, so I already know he's about to spazz the fuck out. Again, I'm sorry." She quickly hugged me and rushed out of the salon.

I could tell my mother was visibly upset, and she should be. Kato's ass done came and ruined a perfectly good damn day. I can't wait to talk to Draylon and ask him about that comment he made. It was as if he knew my father, or they'd had an interaction before.

I'm not sure what it was, but there was something behind what Draylon said. I really am happy my dad came to see me, but at the same time, I would prefer he stayed away if his presence caused drama.

Chapter 6: Belladonna

I'm so mad at myself. I let my emotions get the best of me and acted out of character. Kato isn't even a soft spot for me anymore. It was just the idea of him saying what he said. That man had the audacity to say something about Keizon being young, as if I wasn't young when he got me pregnant. I got a flashback out of this world and attacked his ass. I'm so upset about messing up my daughter's grand opening. Draylon, Keizon, and I had all come to celebrate with her. Shit went left all the way around, and Keizon was now angry as fuck with me. To make matters worse, I'm plastered all over social media for fucking up Kato. It's been a couple of days, and he is still walking around with an attitude. Keizon was taking this shit farther than it had to go.

Since getting married, we have had no fallouts, so this has me kind of fucked up in the head, mainly because I'm not really sure how I'll react if he pisses me off. A bitch might fuck around and started throwing shit at his ass. Let Facebook tell it, I've got a good ass throwing arm.

After a long ass day of doing heads, all I wanted to do was come home and lie down. Pulling up to see La-La's car in my driveway irritated the fuck out of me. For the sake of Keizon and Latasia, I've let bygones be bygones, but at the same time, she still be pissing me the fuck off.

La-La is not fooling me. It's sad as fuck to watch the manipulation. I'm the type of bitch that looks at the bigger picture. The shit is crystal clear, but Tasia and Keizon are too blind to see it. La-La didn't decide to sell that ugly ass trap house until she found out about her kids' affiliation with the Prince family. The money-hungry hoe doesn't see shit but dollar signs. She sold that house so she could get a bigger house, which is exactly what

Keizon's dumb ass just went and did. I'm pissed, but it's not my place to overstep that boundary. Make no mistake, I'm going to tear La-La's ass up if she betrays them. They are really happy about her finally being a mother to them, which is another reason I haven't beaten her ass. In a nutshell, La-La is still a worthless ass mother.

"It's about time your ass made it. Come on, I cooked dinner." La-La greeted me like we were friends.

Now, this heifer should know I'm not eating anything she cooked.

"What the hell are you doing cooking in my kitchen? You had better not have scratched up my granite countertops." I rushed into the kitchen and inspected my countertops.

"Calm down with your bougie ass! Ain't nobody messed up your counters. Come on now, Belladonna. I'm trying to be a good mother-in-law." La-La stated.

I fell the fuck out laughing at hearing this crazy bitch say. Her ass was not my mother-in-law. I don't care if I am married to her son.

"La-La, you are not my mother-in-law. We are the same damn age. I'm not about to be fooling with you. Where is Keizon?"

"His mean ass is upstairs. I don't care what your bougie ass says. You're my daughter-in-law." she insisted.

I waved La-La's crazy ass off and went to talk to my husband. I wondered if he knew his momma had officially lost her fucking mind.

The moment I stepped into our bedroom; my pussy got wet. Keizon was laid out in bed shirtless with a pair of Fendi boxers on. His tattoos were glistening against his chocolate skin. *Damn, my husband is fine with his mean ass.* I quickly removed my shoes and climbed into the bed next to him. Without hesitation, I laid my head on his chest.

"How long you gone be mad at me?"

"Until I don't want to be mad no more. Raise up!" He roughly sat up, causing my head to fall off him.

"Nigga, you got me fucked up. I'm confused as to why you're mad at me. I had no idea Kato was going to grab and kiss me. You, of all people, know I wouldn't do no shit like that to you."

"Let me ask you something. How come you didn't push him off you?"

"Really Keizon? I don't have time for this bullshit!" I tried to walk out of the bedroom, but he roughly yanked me back.

"You gone have time for whatever the fuck I want you to have time for! Let me make myself fucking clear. If another nigga ever invades your fucking space like that again, you better knock that nigga the fuck out! In my opinion, you really didn't check that nigga about the disrespect accordingly. Throwing shit at the nigga got me feeling like you're still in love with him or something. Don't even think about playing with me. I'll murk you and that fuck nigga!"

When I say I was standing there stunned to silence, I was. My feelings were really hurt that Keizon would insinuate that I wanted Kato. If I wasn't pissed off before, I was really pissed off now.

As he got dressed, I took off my clothes and threw on some pajamas. I was mentally exhausted from this drama with him, not to mention physically exhausted from standing on my feet doing hair all day. Honestly, I didn't even have the energy to address his ass. Keizon was going to regret saying that shit to me. He had me fucked up. I was not one of these young bitches. I was not just old and in fucking love. I was far wise beyond my years to let some nigga handle me like that. I was still the baddest bitch who the streets called Belladonna. If Keizon wanted to be mad, I was about to make him madder.

"Are you sure about this, ma?"

"Yes, and don't ask me that shit again!"

Kateevah had been asking me the same question repeatedly. We were chilling at one of my favorite hole-in-the-wall spots. It had been a minute since I'd come out and enjoyed myself. Keizon had been calling me all night, and I wasn't answering for his ass.

"I'm so happy I came out with y'all." Tasia declared as she danced and knocked back a shot.

Her ass was acting like a free damn bird tonight. Clearly, she had to get the hell away from Horse for a minute, too. All I knew was her ass better not have told her brother where the fuck we were.

"It does feel good to be outside for a change. I feel like all I do is work and go home. I'm surprised Draylon hasn't called yet."

"Keizon has been blowing me up, but I'm not going to answer for his ass," I announced.

"Horse hasn't called me once. His ass is probably happy I'm not in the house. As a matter of fact, let me go to the bathroom and check on him. This is his first time alone with the baby. I'm scared he's gone get high and fall asleep on Junior. Horse sleeps hard as fuck. I'll be right back." Tasia informed us.

"I still can't believe that crazy heifer got a baby." I laughed, looking at Tasia in mommy mode.

"I know, right. She's so happy with Horse even though the nigga likes weird ass sex."

"She was telling me Horse done turned her ass out. That's why she be acting all crazy with that man. They definitely belong together." As I spoke, I observed Kato approaching our table. The fact that he was with his wife really irritated me.

"What the fuck do you want, nigga?"

"Calm down, Belladonna. I come in peace. Look, I just want to apologize for the shit I said to you the other day. A nigga was just surprised to hear that you were married. My plan is to be in my daughter's and granddaughter's lives going forward. It would be nice for them to come and visit with us." Kato explained.

"Get the fuck away from this table and take ya bitch with you! I'm not sure what the motive is, but don't play with them. Since when is this bitch wanting my daughter to be around her?" I fumed.

"Please, y'all stop. I'm grown, and I can make my own decisions. I love you, ma, and I love you, daddy. Let's not even do this here."

"That's your momma being ignorant." Kato's wife chimed in.

I came across the table so quick on her ass. She had no

business saying shit to me, not to mention calling me ignorant.

"Let her go, Belladonna!" Kato was trying his best to stop me, but I had a death grip on this bitch with one hand and knocking the shit out of her with the other. The bitch doesn't know me, so she asked for this. I didn't stop fucking her up until I was satisfied.

"Come on, ma. Let's go!" Kateevah urged.

"What the fuck happened? All I did was go to the bathroom." Tasia asked.

"Belladonna, your ass is wrong!" Kato yelled.

"Keep talking to me, and I'll fuck both of y'all up!" I threatened.

Kateevah started pulling me hard as fuck toward the door. I swear it felt like I was the child, and she was the mother. I was mad at myself all over again because I allowed myself to get out of character. The last thing I need is Keizon getting wind of me fighting Kato's wife. He'll definitely thinks I'm pressed about the nigga or something.

"Do not tell your brother about what happened?"

"Now you know I'm not about to tell Keizon shit."

"Let's hurry up and get the fuck out of here. Hopefully, nobody recorded your ass, Belladonna Ali!"

Kateevah and Latasia laughed like some shit was funny. These folks out here are triggering the fuck out of me, and it's looking like I'm the fucking problem. My old ass gone be sore all over again behind tagging that bitch ass. Honestly, I feel like I stood on big business in both situations. Kato and his bitch had that ass whooping coming for playing with my daughter and me for years. Now a bitch has got to figure out how to get shit back on track with my husband.

Chapter 7: Keizon

Belladonna really wanted to see a side of me I don't like to show. Seeing me calling and not answering got a nigga's blood pressure sky-high. I would have been snatched her ass up if I didn't have to handle some important shit. She thinks I don't know her ass was fighting the nigga Kato bitch! That shit really doesn't sit right with me. She's in her feelings but still showing me why I have every right to be mad. It's cool, though, because I will be the first face she sees when she gets in here. My wife has no reason to be out here fighting with nobody. Belladonna is a boss-ass bitch. That's why I fell in love with her. She always carried herself real boss-like. My baby has always been a flawless ass woman. She's the type of BBW skinny bitches wish they could be. I'm not exaggerating, either. Even if a motherfucker disagrees with that. I'm still going to pipe my bitch up, anyway. She's in her forties giving young bitches a run for their money. A nigga can put his best bitches in a lineup against my wife, and all of them hoes will lose.

As you can see, I'm real sprung on Belladonna, so seeing her nut up with another nigga just doesn't sit well in my spirit. I don't give a fuck if he is Kateevah's father. The idea of him disrespecting me got murder on my mind. If that nigga knows like I know, he will tread lightly. I guarantee there are no more passes. One thing I'm not about to play about is Mrs. Keizon Kirkland.

Outside of dealing with my wife, I'm trying to keep a leveled head about this shit with the Russians. A nigga needs to be focused on dealing with them motherfuckers. They have no fucking idea about the war they're about to be in. Draylon is on some different shit, but I'm fucking with it.

"Fuckkk! You scared the shit out of me! Why the fuck you in

here sitting with the lights off?"

"'Cause I knew you were gone try sneaking your ass in here."

"I was not sneaking. From the sound of your tone, I take it you know about what happened. Go ahead and go off!" she sassed.

Belladonna was standing with her hand on her hip, looking good ass fuck with them big pretty ass titties sitting up dying to be sucked on. Speaking of that...

"Why the fuck you got that shirt on? You love showing these niggas two of the biggest reasons they gone get killed."

"Baby, you know none of these niggas out here fucking with you. I don't want anybody but you. I married you. I love you, Keizon. I'm sorry if I disrespected you," she cooed.

This wasn't going the way I wanted. Belladonna was apologizing and undressing at the same time. I'm so fucking obsessed with this woman.

"I love you, too! Look at your beautiful ass! Stop playing! You know you that bitch! I have every right to want to keep you hidden from the world. Fuckkkkk!" I moaned out as Belladonna deep-throated my dick. She knew how to get me to shut the fuck up. I swear to God!

| | | | |

A Couple of Days Later

La-La hadn't been around in a couple of days, and I had grown concerned. It wasn't like her to just do disappearing acts and not answer. Since we reconciled our differences, she had become a permanent fixture in my and my sister's lives. We loved having her around. It felt like we had the old La-La back. I was lowkey worried about her, so I had to stop by her new spot to check on her. I was happy as fuck she had given me a key. Since she wasn't answering, I decided to just go inside. Her car was out front, which had me spooked like a motherfucker. That means she was here, and I'm hoping she hadn't died or no shit like that. Then again, La-La's scandalous ass is going to outlive all of us. Don't get me wrong, I see the effort. At the same time, I know that selfish motherfucker still lives inside her. I had to forgive my mother because you only get one. All I can do is hope she's genuinely trying to repair our bond.

I carried my gun down to my side as I walked through the house. Her room was in the back, so I headed down the hallway. The sound of her voice made me speed up. Without knocking, I walked inside the room.

"Oh shit, it's Keizon!" La-La screamed. She was lying in the bed and quickly jumped up.

For a minute, I stood speechless, looking at my father Lynwood, the same father who was supposed to be dead.

"Son."

"Don't touch me. I'll blow your fucking head off!" I gritted, raising the gun, and pointed it in his face.

"Calm down, Keizon! Let me explain!"

"There ain't shit to explain! The both of y'all are some sick motherfuckers. I really hate that me and my fucking sister come from you."

"Listen to me, son! You have to get away from the Prince family. They're dangerous. I'm supposed to be in Witness Protection but left the program hearing your fucking sister had a baby with one of them motherfuckers. To make matters worse, you're working for them! I'm still your father, Keizon, so put that fucking gun down and listen to what I'm saying."

I looked at this nigga like he had lost his fucking mind. It was imperative I get the fuck out of here. The urge to kill them was consuming me.

"You stopped being my father the moment you left. Nigga, fuck you!"

"Keizon!"

"Fuck you too, La-La!"

I punched a hole in the bedroom wall before leaving. This shit was not real, and it couldn't be happening. Just when life is good for Tasia and me, this shit comes to light! I can't believe this shit. How in the fuck am I supposed to tell my sister that our father was alive?

The Next Morning

"Keizon, you need to get up, baby!" The sound of Belladonna's voice made my head hurt worse than it was. After finding that shit out yesterday, all I could do was get fucked up.

"What time is it?"

"Eight in the morning. You told me to wake you up because you had some business to handle. Are you hungry?"

"Draylon changed the meetup time to later tonight, so we're good. Come lay with me for a little while, Belladonna."

"Is everything okay?" The feeling of her wrapping her arms around me felt good as fuck. Some niggas don't even be knowing that all they need is a hug from they woman.

"My father is alive." I disclosed.

"That's not funny, Keizon."

"I'm serious, babe. Yesterday, I went to check on La-La because I hadn't heard from her. When I went inside her house, I found her and my father in bed together. I'm dead ass serious. My father is alive, and La-La knew. Why she got to be so fucked up as a mother?"

"Because the bitch is a fucked-up person. La-La is selfish as fuck. I'm about to go whoop her ass!" Belladonna jumped up from the bed and started putting on her clothes.

"Nah! It's cool. Just chill."

"Hell nah! That shit is wrong. Just like you don't play about me, I don't play about you. What type of wife would I be if I let people hurt you? It's bad enough that La-La's the reason you went back to jail. You forgave her ass, and she's still doing fucked-up shit. This is so unacceptable, Keizon! I'm going to kick her ass the moment I see her." Belladonna was snapping, and I knew there was no stopping her.

Instead of going back and forth with her, I handled my personal hygiene and got ready to talk to Latasia. I had to let her know what the fuck I had witnessed. There was no way I couldn't tell my sister this shit, even though I really didn't want to.

"Come here, baby."

"You're not going to be able to talk me out of fucking La-La up!"

"Listen, Belladonna, you have to allow me to handle my

mother my way. Baby, I'm flattered that you love me the way you do. I've never experienced love like this. I appreciate it. This shit is sensitive, and I need to handle it accordingly. You see, my father said we needed to get away from the Prince family. I need to get down to the bottom of all of that.

"I'm not liking this at all, Keizon. Whatever beef your father had was with Draylon and Horse's father, not with you. I think you should talk to them about this. Are you going to talk to your father?"

"Yeah, but first, I want to talk to Tasia. She needs to know that he's alive."

"I don't think you should do that. At least talk to your father first. I'm not sure it's a good thing to tell Tasia. She just had the baby, and she's happy with Horse right now. Even though they be about to kill each other, you know she loves him. Horse is the best thing that has happened to her, especially after that Rico situation. I know that you're going to move the way you choose but just think about it. I'm going to go downstairs and cook you something." She kissed me on the lips and left me alone with my thoughts.

It didn't feel right not telling Latasia, but at the same time, Belladonna was right. My sister was happy. Learning that our father was really alive will fuck her up. I'm going to take my wife's advice and talk with my father first. It's imperative I do that before having a sit down with Draylon and Horse.

Chapter 8: Draylon

"Thanks for seeing me, Draylon." Nautica stated as she stepped into my office.

Nautica had been reaching out to see me since she'd popped up at the crib. However, out of respect for my wife, I declined all of her calls. I wasn't sure what she wanted to talk about, seeing as though it had been years since I had seen her. While behind bars, she was taken great care of. I'd long ago detached myself from her. Draya was the one who ensured she kept money on the books and visited her every couple of months. I'm sure she wants to talk so she could ask for money, which I'm more than willing to give her. Nautica had lost her freedom to save us, so it's only right that I make sure she can live good in the free world. I'm positive Kateevah won't be able to accept me doing anything for her financially. However, she'll have to understand. This is more about business than it is personal.

"It's cool. Have a seat? I'm about to pour myself a drink. Would you like something?" I offered.

"Yeah. I'll have whatever you're having."

I headed over to the wet bar and poured us some shots of Don Julio.

"Now tell me, Nautica, why have you been wanting to talk to me?"

"This shit ain't right, Draylon."

"You gone have to elaborate on that statement."

"Draya and Mr. Prince are dead. The crazy part is that no one seems to remember having a funeral service. As a matter of fact, the streets are saying they think you killed them because they went against you. Please tell me that's not the truth."

Before answering Nautica's question, I knocked back my shot

and poured myself another.

"You are an honorary member of this family. You aren't kin to us by blood, so personal Prince family business is something that I won't be discussing. I'm not really sure what answers you were expecting, especially when it's none of your concern. My father and my sister met with an untimely demise in the same streets that you say are talking. You and I both know this visit is about something bigger than them. I'm sorry that I didn't wait for you. Life went on for me. I'm sympathetic that life for you came to a halt when you had to go away. Believe me when I tell you that shit doesn't go unappreciated. That's why I wanted to give you some bread for your troubles. It will be more than enough for you to live comfortably for the rest of your life. Give me a number, and we can make it happen."

"I don't want your fucking money, Draylon. All I want is you. That's all I ever wanted. It was you who promised me we would be together forever. Since the day I gave you my virginity, I've been in love with you. As I sat in that jail cell, all I thought about was coming home to you and living the life you owe me!" Nautica professed.

"I don't owe you a life. As a matter of fact, I don't owe you shit. I'm married. Just give me a number, Nautica! You're sitting here crying for nothing. Come on now. You're behaving unrealistically. There is no way you thought you were coming home to me. I'm sorry, but you and I will never be. Honestly, there was never an us to begin with." I leveled with her.

I wasn't trying to hurt her feelings. She just needed to hear the truth.

"Draya always said you were a heartless motherfucker, but I never wanted to believe her because you were always a good person. At least you used to be, anyway. Who the fuck are you? Nigga, you are not the Draylon I fell in love with."

"That's because he's the Draylon that fell in love with me!" Kateevah interjected.

"What you are doing here, Kateevah?" My heart sped up a little, seeing my wife step inside my office. A nigga was definitely about to be in the doghouse. She was pissed.

"Girl, bye! It ain't that deep!"

"Yet you're here, begging my husband to love you. That's so unfortunate!"

"What's unfortunate is you trying to act like you're that bitch! Newsflash, you aren't! You and your daughter ain't shit but pawns to the Prince family. Any and everybody that comes around them becomes expendable. Do you think this nigga magically appeared and gave you this luxury life? The only reason you have it is because I was away. I'm back now, and I'm not going anywhere!" Nautica spewed.

"Bitch, that can be arranged!" Kateevah yelled.

"I came here with peace, but since you motherfuckers are choosing violence, let's do it. I came here looking for Draya because she knows where my son is!"

"What, son! What the fuck are you talking about?"

"I'm talking about our son Draylon Prince Jr.! He's nine years old, and your sister has had him since I gave birth in jail. Here are all the documents and pictures. Nigga, this ain't about me and you! It's about our son. Ask your mother and your grandmother. They know all about him but are refusing to give him to me. I swear to God, if I don't get my son back, I'm going to tell the world that the Prince family are kidnappers!" Nautica threatened.

She rushed out of the office crying before I could say anything to her.

I stood speechless, looking at the documents and the pictures. Shock consumed me to the point where I was damn near shaking. A nigga needed to take a seat. Looking at my sister's signature on the paperwork solidified that Nautica was telling the truth. I felt like I wanted to shed tears looking at the pictures of my son. No DNA test was needed. He and Unique looked like twins.

Kateevah walked over and snatched the paperwork out of my hand.

"Baby! I swear to God. I didn't know. Please don't leave me!" I was holding onto my wife for dear life. This was something that would be hard for Kateevah to accept.

"I would never leave you for something like this. If that's your son, I want nothing more than for you to be in his life. I'm a mother, so I would never take my anger out on him. However, I'll kill his mother about you. That hoe is not fooling me. She would do whatever to get Unique and me out of the way. That shit will never happen. Nigga, you gone leave this world being my husband. Now, let's go!" Kateevah was yelling and acting crazy.

"Where the fuck are we going, Kateevah?" She was pulling me like I was her son. I needed to yank away from her nutty ass so she could unhand me.

"We're about to go see your ain't shit momma and granny! This bitch just came in here and said they know about him. There is no need to be waiting around thinking about your next move. Let's go, Draylon!"

"Aye! Pipe the fuck down! I understand you're mad, but don't forget who the fuck the boss is around this bitch! Don't yell at me and watch your fucking tone going forward!" I warned. I didn't mean to come at her so hard. However, I'm the man in this relationship. She doesn't tell me what the fuck to do, especially not like this.

"Don't talk to me like that, nigga! I'm your wife, not one of your fucking foot soldiers!"

Kateevah walked out of the office, and I didn't bother to go behind her. It wasn't because I didn't want to. What I said to her wasn't cool, so I needed to fall back and check myself. This shit cannot be happening right now. At the moment, I was regretting killing the bitch, Draya. The hoe was still going against me from the pits of hell. What type of bitch ass people have my family turned into?

Growing up, I would never have thought in a million years that our family would be like this. My mother and grandmother have really disappointed me. For a minute, I thought they were ten toes down for me. Now I know they can't be trusted either. Hopefully, I don't have to kill them, but I will if they leave me no choice. The fact that they have been lying in my face for years speaks volumes about the level motherfuckers would go to keep secrets.

I was confused as to why they thought they didn't have to tell me. I would have never been out here living life knowing that Nautica had birthed my seed. This shit had me feeling even more fucked up than when I learned about my daughter. My mother and grandmother had really better hope it's not true that they've known this shit. My blood was boiling, and my trigger finger was itching. I was fed the fuck up with the betrayals, and I was on the verge of crashing the fuck out.

There was too much at stake for me to lose control and murk them. Honestly, I didn't want to. Killing Draya and my father haunted me daily, so I'd be fucked up mentally if I had to off them, too. I really did love them both. However, they were consistently showing me that they weren't with me. I simply couldn't accept that shit. Hopefully, they'd have a good ass reason why they would keep something like this away from me. I'm not excluding the bitch Nautica either because she knew too.

Before heading to talk to my mother and grandmother, I tried calling Kateevah in the hopes that she would come with me. Of course, she didn't answer. A nigga was definitely in the doghouse. My baby Kateevah is so soft and pure. I know I can't be yelling and talking to her like that. Now, I have to figure out how to apologize, not to mention reassure her that life is not about to change for us. The shit will be better. Life with me will always be greater. I just need her to trust in my word. I'll never lead my wife in the wrong direction. She just needs to understand I'm not some regular ass nigga, so the way she speaks and handles a nigga needs to be different.

Hours Later

"How come you didn't call and let me know you were coming over? I would have cooked something," my mother stated as she let me inside her new house.

My brother and I had purchased her all new everything. Since completing rehab, there has been nothing she can't get from us.

She stepped inside, and I followed close behind her into the kitchen.

"This is not a fucking social call, ma. Nautica came by today talking about how we have a son together! The bitch says you and Granny knew about this shit. All of this time, ma! You and Draya have been in on this bullshit the whole time. Like, what the fuck? Why is my fucking family against me?" I ranted.

"First of all, calm the fuck down! I'm not an angel, and I've done my dirt. However, I would never keep something like that from you. Second of all, the bitch Nautica knows neither me nor your grandmother knew anything about it until after Draya was gone."

"So, what the fuck is really going on, then?"

"Granny hired a moving company to pack up Draya's things to be placed in storage. She gathered up all business and personal documents. Going through the shit, she found the fucking birth certificate. Nautica did give birth to your son behind bars. There's a problem, though."

"What's that?'

"Draya gave him up for adoption. She's been lying to Nautica all this time, saying she had him put away safely, but the whole time that crazy bitch had given him to strangers. I'll never understand why Nautica or Draya didn't think they could tell you this. Draylon, I didn't tell you because we've been trying to find him. If I'm guilty of anything, it's trying to protect you from that hurt. I swear we're going to find him."

I sat across from my mother, trying not to blow up. Her eyes showed me she was telling the truth. I'm not even mad that she kept it from me after finding out about it. Clearly, the bitch Draya has been against me from the jump. She's dead, and I have no regrets. Still, all I can do is wonder what I did to her. The love I had for my sister was top-tier, and there was nothing I wouldn't do for her. There aren't a lot of things that hurt me, but this really has me shedding internal tears.

"Stop looking for him." I declared.

"What? Draylon, we can't just leave him out in the world with strangers!" my mother countered.

"Nautica is going to find him. It's her fucking fault he's with strangers, anyway. Had she come to me from the jump, we wouldn't be discussing this right now. That bitch has a lot of nerve thinking she's going to come here and demand some shit, not to mention throwing threats, talking about she's going to tell the world we're kidnappers. I advise you and Granny to sit that bitch down and have a talk with her. If I see her again, I'll shoot that bitch in her face. Oh yeah, call Kateevah. Tell her everything you just told me."

"You're in the doghouse, huh?"

"Hell yeah. She was there when Nautica revealed that shit. Now she's under the impression that you and Granny knew. Be careful, ma. I think Kateevah wants to tussle with you and Granny."

"I'm not scared of your crazy ass wife, but at the same time, I'm not trying to tussle with her ass either. Kateevah is really crazy behind you. When Nautica showed up, I saw murder in her eyes. I'm telling you, son, you need to keep your eyes on her ass. I'll talk to her tomorrow when I go pick up Unique. Don't worry about Nautica. I'll handle that lil' messy bitch. She has another thing coming if she thinks she's about to get some shit started. I'll kill her ass myself before I let that happen."

I got a good look at my mother as she spoke about killing Nautica, and the look in her eyes let me know that she was capable of doing it. My mother be trying to lowkey act like she's not really with the shit but supports me. That's a bunch of bullshit. Yeah, she'll agree with me, but I know she's capable of anything. My mother didn't bat an eye when she realized I was torturing my father and my sister. She didn't even show a hint of sadness. That was alarming to me. I thought she would at least feel some type of way about losing her husband and her daughter.

Honestly, I really don't understand why she has supported my decision to kill them. Some days, I feel like she has the ability to cross me, but then there are days where I feel like she's ten toes down. Either way, I have to keep my eyes on her and my slick-ass granny. Neither one of them can be fully trusted. I'm just happy

I know she's telling the truth. God knows I didn't wake up this morning with the intention of killing their asses.

| | | | |

The Next Day

"Are you sure the bitch Nautica is not lying?" Horse asked as he flamed up a blunt. We were sitting at my crib in the man cave.

"Nah, Granny and Ma confirmed the shit through the paperwork. Hell, I saw the paperwork. The shit is legit. I'm just having a hard time coming to terms with why Draya wouldn't come and tell me that. Honestly, I'm fucked up in the head all the way around. I keep trying to figure out what I did to her."

If I sounded sad, it's because I was. I've always made sure never to show weakness in front of my brother. We're not wired that way. However, I feel I have the right to express my real feelings behind this shit.

"Listen, bro, don't even stress yourself out about that shit. Fuck Draya! We'll never know why she went against the grain. All we can do is make sure she doesn't fuck us over in the afterlife. Draya and Pops hurt the fuck out of my heart, so trust me when I tell you that I know how you feel. Just know you're my big brother, and I love you. I'll never go against you. I'll lay down and die for you. That's on my son. Listen, you're the boss of all bosses. The king of this fucking city. Don't shit move unless you say so. We're the Prince family, and we can't be fucked with. You did what the fuck you had to do. Stop walking around feeling fucked up about that. Focus on this move we're about to do with Nikolov."

"Say less! I needed to hear that, lil' bro. For the record, you're the one nigga I know I can trust. Don't ever think I thought you could move fucked up with me. I'm going to let this shit with Draya go. The shit is just crazy as fuck to me. I have a whole fucking son somewhere living with strangers. The bitch Nautica knew she could tell me, yet her dumb ass let Draya get in her head. What do you think I should do about that hoe? I got a bad vibe from her. The bitch got weird energy, and I'm not feeling it."

"Snatch her ass up and make her talk. Nautica and Draya were best friends, so there is no way that bitch doesn't know anything about the whereabouts of her baby. We need to get at her before she jumps ship."

"You know what? You're right. I want you and Keizon to handle that for me ASAP!"

"We got you. I'm going to go ahead and get up out of here. I have to go meet up with Diwanna."

"Are you sure that's a good idea? Tasia is going to kill your ass, bro."

"I'm not on no bullshit. I just feel like Diwanna needs to actually hear it from my mouth that we're done. The bitch has been beating my line down. This is the third phone I've had to purchase this week. Tasia keeps going through my phone and breaking it. I'm not entertaining no hoes. I've really been on my faithful nigga shit, but Tasia is making the shit hard. I'll hit your line when we have Nautica put up. Love you, big bro."

"Love you too." We hugged and dapped it up."

Once Horse left, I sat and got higher than a giraffe's pussy. A nigga needed to relax. I have more than enough bullshit on my plate. It's merely small shit to a motherfucking giant. The higher I got, the harder my dick got. I took a couple of shots of tequila and went in search of my wife. Unique was gone with my mother, so we were alone.

When I stepped inside our bedroom, Kateevah was fully dressed.

"Where are you going?"

"I'm about to meet some friends for brunch."

"Look, I know you call yourself being mad at me. However, don't tell me you're going out with some friends when I know your only friends are Latasia and your mother. Stop fucking playing with me. Who the fuck are you going to brunch with?" I didn't mean to step into her face, but she was playing with me.

"With some of the stylists at the salon. My mother is not feeling too good, and Latasia is home with the baby. I'm bored."

"So, just because you're bored, you're going to go out with your fucking employees? That's not a good look. There is no way you should be hanging out with people who work for you. Be professional, Kateevah! Now call them and let them know you can't make it. All you had to do was let your nigga know you were bored. We can spend the day together, and I'm not taking no for an answer. Change what the fuck you got on and put on something sexier. I don't want to hear no fucking back talk either." I demanded, grabbing her by the throat and shoving my tongue into her mouth.

"I'm not your child, Draylon," Kateevah protested.

I ignored the fuck out of her and got dressed. One thing I wasn't about to do was go back and forth with Kateevah. Of course, I know she's not my child.

Kateevah has a lot to learn about running a business. She shouldn't be hanging out with people that she does business with. She shouldn't be talking about going out to brunch with strangers just because she's bored. That's how motherfuckers get their drinks and shit spiked. I would lose my mind if some shit like that happened to her.

Kateevah has to get in tune with who she is and who the fuck she's married to. All it takes is for an enemy to see her out so freely walking around, and they'll snatch her up quick. I'll never forgive myself if something like that happened. It's imperative she stops being green and uses her common sense. Going out with random people is something she should know she shouldn't be doing.

Chapter 9: Kateevah

I'm not going to even lie. It feels good as fuck to be kicking it with my husband, which is exactly what I wanted to do. The petty part of me didn't want to just ask him to take me out, so I faked it like I was going out with the stylists. I knew he would never go for that shit. The nigga fell right into my trap. Honestly, I'm still in my feelings about the way he spoke to me at his office. That shit really rubbed me the wrong way. Besides that, I still feel some way about that bitch Nautica. There is something about that bitch that doesn't sit right with me.

Before walking into Draylon's office, I overheard her talking about him and her being together. Her initial conversation had nothing to do with having a son. I'm confused as to why she didn't tell Draylon they shared a kid when she first showed up at the house. Leave it to that snake-ass Draya to be in on some shit like this.

As I sit across from my husband, I can't help but wonder how he feels. He always puts on such a brave front, but I'm positive Draylon is hurt. I can see it in his eyes, and I feel so sorry for him. All I want to do is make everything better for him. Learning that Draya basically gave his child away hurt me. How could you do that to someone?

"Thank you for spending the day with me." I leaned across the table and kissed him on the lips.

"You don't have to thank me. It feels good to spend the day with you. We barely get to do that. We can have date night every week going forward. Just let me know in advance what you want to do."

"Are you serious, Draylon?" I was looking at his ass with questionable eyes. This man is all about his business twenty-four-seven.

"Hell yeah. I don't want you to feel like I don't have time for you, so I will make sure I always make time for you. I'm sorry for raising my voice at you."

"It's okay. I know you didn't mean it. Let's go home. We have the house to ourselves, so we can fuck all around the house if we want to."

"Our house is big ass fuck, Kateevah! You think you can hang with a nigga that long?"

"I've become very accustomed to that dick. You know I can handle it like a pro now. Don't do me, Draylon."

"Come on, let's head out then. I want you to remind me how you can handle this motherfucker."

Draylon threw stacks of one-hundred-dollar bills on the table, grabbing my hand and leading me out of the restaurant. He was walking so damn fast. It was hard for me to keep up. My ass had on some damn high heels and was bound to bust my shit.

"Slow down, Draylon! Baby, you see I got these damn heels on," I fussed.

Draylon stopped walking and turned around to kiss me. I was taken aback by that. He dropped down to my feet and started undoing the strap around my ankle. It took me right back to the first night we met. When he gestured for me to get on his back, I wanted to cry. I'm not going to lie. I was about to say that I was too heavy, but I knew it would piss him off, so I decided to just go with the flow. As he carried me on his back, I silently thanked God for him. I'm positive there isn't another nigga out here breathing that will love me this way. This is some top-tier type of loving, and I love that for me.

The Next Day

After a long ass night of fucking, I had finally found the strength to get out of bed. Draylon had fucked the shit out of me. My whole damn body was hurting, but I felt so good at the same time. I enjoyed everything about our date. I'm happy he told me we would have more dates. I plan on putting together some great date night ideas.

My phone started to ring, so I quickly grabbed it from the nightstand. I rolled my eyes, seeing that it was from my father. He had been trying his best to get me to come over to his house. Honestly, I had been avoiding him because I wasn't sure my mother would be okay with that. Then again, I know she wouldn't care as long as his ass doesn't let us down. Then again, he won't do that because I don't need him for shit. I would love to have a solid father/daughter relationship with him. However, I'm okay if we don't. I can't miss anything I've never really had.

Kato: *Hey, baby girl. Call your pops back when you get a chance.*
Me: *Okay.*

I wasn't in the mood to talk to him right now, so I'm going to call him back later. Hearing Annalise's voice irritated me. I'm still pissed off about her knowing Nautica had a baby by Draylon. She should have told Draylon the moment she found out. I'm mad at Granny's old ass, too, for giving that bitch our address. I swear I get a bad vibe about that bitch.

"Hey, mommy!" Unique ran full speed and wrapped her arms around my waist.

"What's up, daughter? Did you have fun with your grandma?"

"Yes! I know how to play Spades now!"

"Really, Annalise? You should be teaching her how to play Go Fish, not no Spades." Something is truly wrong with the Prince family and their way of parenting. These folks have no clue about raising kids.

"Oh please, Kateevah! Go Fish ain't gone help her in this life. You got to know how to play Spades in the Black community. It's a part of our culture. It's not like I'm gambling with her like Horse ignorant ass. Go upstairs for a minute, Unique. Let me talk to your momma."

I should have known Annalise would find some type of justification. There was so much I wanted to say about it, but I kept my mouth closed. Talking to these folks is a waste of time. I'll never get used to the bad habits they teach my daughter.

"So, what's up, Annalise? What do you want to talk about?" I poured myself a glass of wine and waited for her to start talking.

"I know your crazy ass calls yourself mad at Granny and me, but we didn't know anything about Nautica having a kid with Draylon. We found out going through Draya's thing. I'll tell you just like I told Draylon. The only reason I didn't tell him about it was because I wanted to find his son first. That bitch Nautica flat-out lied, trying to make it like we knew some shit."

"How much do you love her, Annalise? I mean, you did adopt her."

"I also gave birth to Draya and could give a fuck less about the little bitch being dead. Nautica is nothing to me, so you don't have to question it. In my eyes, she's a snake. All of this time, she hid the fact that she had a son who had the Prince's blood running through his veins. I don't trust the bitch either. One thing for sure and two for certain. I can assure you I'm team Draylon, so please stop questioning my and Granny's loyalty."

"I don't mean any disrespect, Annalise. However, I will always question Draylon's family's loyalty. I've seen how people have crossed and hurt him. Draylon is a good man, and he loves his family. He loves this family so much that he goes out every day and puts his life on the line. He gives out so much love, so I want to always ensure he gets that love back. My husband doesn't deserve to ever be crossed again. As long as I'm his wife, I'm going to go above and beyond to ensure that doesn't happen," I vowed.

"I'm happy that you're passionate about taking care of Draylon. As I said, you don't have to worry about me hurting him or crossing him, for that matter. As his wife, you have every right to protect your husband. As his mother, I have the right to protect him in any way I see fit. Are we good?" Annalise responded.

"We are great. Just do me a favor and keep me in the loop about all things Nautica. Your loyalty is to me, too! I mean, after all, I know who really killed Shameeka."

"Oh yeah? Who really killed her? All of this time, I've been under the impression it was Draya."

Fuckkkkkkk! I thought to myself.

Draylon walked into the kitchen while I was running off at

my fucking mouth. I didn't even hear him come inside the house. Both me and Annalise were looking like a deer in headlights.

"Answer me, Kateevah!" Draylon yelled and started walking toward me. I was scared shitless because he had morphed into mean ass Draylon that quick.

"No! It was me, son. I'm the one who killed Shameeka. That bitch had ruined my daughter and betrayed you. I went to y'all house to tell her she needed to leave the Prince family. I no longer wanted her around the family. She started talking shit, so I decided to kill her ass. I put some horse tranquilizers in her wine glass. Once I knew she was dead. I cut her fucking head off." Annalise interjected.

I was shocked hearing her reveal how she had killed Shameeka. For the first time, I saw the bitch was a couple of bricks short of a building. Her eyes were cold and calculating, and the smirk on her face showed me that she enjoyed killing Shameeka's ass.

"I guess you did that for me too, huh?"

"Yes, I did. I am not sorry, nor do I have any regrets. If you're going to be mad at anybody, be mad at me. Kateevah had no idea until I told her."

Now why did this bitch have to put the focus back on me?

"How long have you known?" he gritted in my direction.

"Huh?" That was all my dumb, scared ass could say. Of course, I heard him loud and clear.

"I'm only going to ask you one more time. How fucking long have you known?" Draylon repeated as he pushed Annalise out of his way and got up in my face.

"I've known since the day I unexpectedly came to the house. Please don't be mad at me!" I confessed.

"Yeah, don't be mad at Kateevah. Be mad at me." Annalise was really pleading on behalf but by Draylon's facial expression. I knew he was pissed.

"I'm mad at both of y'all because you should have told me. Maybe I wouldn't have killed my fucking sister had I known she wasn't the one who killed my wife. You had no right to do that, ma!

The fucking police interrogated me like a motherfucker. It's crazy how you keep saying you're doing shit to protect me, yet it seems like you're really making moves for your own personal reasons, which is fucked up!" he fumed before directing his anger toward me.

"I'm really disappointed in you, Kateevah! For a damn near a year, you've looked me in the face and held a secret. You're always walking around here talking about how down you are for me, yet the whole time, you're against me, too! You talk all this shit about my mother, but you're one and the same — two lying ass motherfuckers!"

"Wait, Draylon! It's not the way you're taking it!" I defended.

"Take your fucking hands off of me before I forget I love you!"

"No! I'm not going to let you go! You can't just walk away without giving me a chance to explain." I voiced, not backing down.

"Fuck you and your explanation, Kateevah!" He yanked away from me so hard that it hurt my long ass nails.

The hurt I felt inside was indescribable. I wanted to burst into tears but couldn't let Annalise see me weak, so I held my tears in. Hearing Draylon peel out of the driveway made my heart sink. The last thing I wanted him to do was leave. It felt like he wasn't coming back.

"Don't worry. He'll come around. He's just mad right now. You know he can't stay mad at you for too long." Annalise advised.

"This time is different, and you know it, Annalise." I stated before walking away from her and heading to my bedroom, making sure to close and lock my door behind me.

I shed tears like a motherfucker because my ass couldn't stomach the idea of Draylon being mad at me. I feel weak ass fuck, right now. Like, I should really be stronger than what I'm being. It's not the end of the world. However, it feels like it is. I just want the love story, not the trials and tribulations that go with it.

A Few Days Later

Sick, sad, and depressed was the best way I could describe how

I felt. Draylon had never returned to the house or answered the phone for me. Still, he was talking to our daughter on a regular basis, and I'm okay with that. Had he been ignoring both of us, I would definitely be about to lose my fucking mind. Thank God, I have been swamped with heads and running the nail salon. However, walking around acting as though nothing is wrong is starting to get to me.

"It's about time your ass made it." Tasia commented as she let me inside her house.

I had been holding everything in and needed someone to talk to. I didn't even want to burden her or my momma with this drama. Sometimes I like to keep shit to myself and try figuring it out on my own.

"I'm sorry. I had a last-minute booking. Where's my god baby?"

"Granny wanted to keep Junior, so I gladly packed his spoiled ass a bag. She and Annalise be sitting up spoiling him, and now I can't get him to stop crying. All Junior wants is to be held, and his fat ass is heavy. I needed a damn break, anyway. Come on, let's get drunk."

"I'm not really in the mood."

"What? Why? Your ass has been acting weird all week. Is you cool, bitch?"

"Not really. Draylon found out I knew his momma was the one who really killed Shameeka. Now he's mad at both of us. The nigga hasn't been home in damn near a week, and I'm really about to lose my fucking mind."

"You bullshitting?"

"I wish the fuck I was. Draylon hurt the fuck out of my feelings. To make matters worse, he won't answer the phone for me. I think he's going to leave me, Tasia." My voice cracked, and tears fell from my eyes. I quickly wiped my face.

"Oh, please! Cut the damn dramatics. That man is not going to leave you. He loves the fuck out of you. Draylon is just feeling betrayed. That's all. You know these Prince niggas are real fucking sensitive. We can ride over to his spot and bust his windows if you want. He will never know it was us." Tasia suggested.

I fell out laughing because I knew her ass was dead serious.

"Hell nah, I don't want to do that. All I want is for him to talk to me so I can explain. Do you think you can talk to Horse and tell him to get Draylon to talk to me?"

"Hell no, I'm not telling my brother shit." Horse chimed in. "Just give him some space. That nigga pissed, sis. He's really in a different mode, a mode that you don't ever want to witness. Just fall back and let him calm down. We have this move to make, and he needs to focus. You and Ma have really fucked him up in the head. Oh yeah, going forward, I'll be running interference between y'all. Don't worry. He'll come around." Horse wrapped his arm around me and gave me a brotherly hug before walking out of the kitchen and leaving us alone.

"I'll talk to him if you want me to, friend." Tasia offered.

"No, the fuck you won't! Mind your business, Tasia!" Horse yelled from the other room.

"Mind your business, Tasia!" she mocked him, which made me laugh a little.

"As much as I would love to have you help me, I don't want you and that nut into it. Let's just get drunk so I can go home and cry myself to sleep." I stated.

That's exactly what my ass was going to do. Draylon was being so extra. I'm not surprised, and I honestly shouldn't be in my feelings. I knew there was a possibility he would go off if he ever found out.

"Girl, please. I'm not paying him or you any attention. Draylon's ass had better not do the most. He knows how sensitive you are."

"Draylon doesn't care, and I know he's not done doing the most. I'll just have to be stronger than I've been. There isn't any time for that sensitive shit. I'm going to take my punches and give him the space he obviously wants."

I sat and kicked it with Latasia for a couple of hours before heading back home. Unique was with my mother, and my ass hated being in that big ass house by myself. The moment I climbed in the bed. I decided to text Draylon in the hopes he would respond.

Me: *I love and miss you so much. I'm sorry I didn't tell you. You know that I would never betray you. Please come home so we can talk.*

After pressing send, I waited anxiously to see if he would respond. About ten minutes later, a text came through from him. As I read it, I regretted texting him.

Draylon: *To be honest, there ain't really shit to talk about. I'm going to stay at one of the other properties for a while. Call Horse if you need anything.*

Me: *Horse is not my husband! You are!*

Draylon: *I'm not so sure you're my wife! So, for now, our marriage is on the shelf.*

Reading that last text made me pull my nightgown up over my face. My eyes filled to the brim with tears and flowed out like a river. What the fuck did he mean by our marriage was on the shelf? Like, what type of shit is that to say to your wife? I threw my phone on the side of me and buried myself underneath my covers. Never in my life have I cried this hard. As tears streamed down my face, I stared at my massive wedding ring. The urge to take it off consumed me. It scared the fuck out of me to think that my marriage might really be over. For Draylon to say that our marriage was on the shelf spoke volumes. The delusional obsessed part of me said it wasn't over, so I wasn't taking my ring off.

| | | | |

Ruth Chris Steakhouse

"Thanks, baby girl. I'm glad you came. I was hoping you brought my grandbaby with you. Here, this is for you, and this is for her." My father handed me two big pink gift bags.

"She's actually with her dad today. You didn't have to get us anything," I lied.

Draylon had come and got her over a week ago and never brought her back home. We have talked daily, so I'm not mad. I'm hurt more than anything. It feels like he abandoned me, and that shit is eating me up. Had I not been swamped with heads to do and running the nail spa, I would be in bed all day crying my eyes out. Staying busy had been helping me keep my mind occupied.

"Yes, I did. Open your gift." Kato's eagerness made me quickly go inside the gift bag. My eyes widened at seeing nothing but stacks of money.

"Why are you giving me all of this money?"

"I've never really done anything like this for you, so I just felt like giving you and my grandbaby fifty thousand a piece. Yeah, I know your husband is rich, and you have your own money. However, more won't hurt."

"You really didn't have to do this, daddy. Thank you. I'm going to put it all toward Unique's college education." I got up and walked around the table to give him a hug.

"Yes, I did. There is more where that came from. I know money can't suffice the times I've let you down. Just know I will not turn my back on you and my granddaughter. I'm going to show your crazy ass momma, and she's gone regret putting her hands on me like that. Belladonna gone see I wasn't on no bullshit."

"Y'all are both crazy. I'm happy I came to have dinner with you. If you don't mind, can I ask you something?" With everything that had been going on, I never got the chance to ask Draylon if he knew my father.

"You can ask me anything."

The server was placing our food in front of us, so I waited until she walked away.

"How do you and Draylon know each other? That day, when I introduced you to each other, it seemed like you knew each other." I started eating some of my food while waiting for him to answer/

"I take he didn't tell you." He grinned.

"No. He didn't tell me anything. That's why I'm asking you."

"Listen, Kateevah. Under any other circumstance, I wouldn't even be about to elaborate on my ties to your husband and his organization. However, you're my daughter, so it's only right I tell you the real. I was real good friends with his pops. We did business together over the years. Recently, my pipeline was cut off by your husband. Draylon doesn't trust anyone who was cool with his pops, so he's no longer doing business with me anymore, which is cool because it's time for me to retire, anyway. I'm not trying to go to war with that nigga. I done got too old for that shit. Plus, knowing that he's married to you and the father of my granddaughter, there is no way I'll do anything to put y'all in harm's way. Just do me a favor and never cross that man, which I don't think you will. It's clear Draylon loves you, and you love him. However, I know his pops and his sister didn't just walk away from the family. The way they were plotting against that man is crazy. It's fucked up that all of this time, I never knew that he was who you had a baby by. That's why I made that statement the way I did. There ain't no beef between Draylon and me. Nor do I want it to be. All I want is for you and my granddaughter to be safe." my father explained.

"Draylon is nothing short of a protector. He will never hurt us. I love him and crossing him is something I would never do just because I know he comes from fucked up people. I hope you really do have the best intentions for us. Anybody who is friends with his father has got to have some fucked up ways."

"You misheard what I said. I said we did business together. I never said anything about us being friends. Your daddy doesn't have friends. I have associates whom I make money with. I'm not a saint, but I'm nothing like Drayton Prince. I love you, Kateevah baby."

"I love you too, daddy."

I'm so glad that it wasn't really anything bad. Lord knows I have enough on my plate with the drama going on. The last thing I needed was there to be beef between my father and my husband. I mean, I think the nigga's still my husband.

Just thinking of Draylon made me so sad. Although I enjoyed the time I was spending with my father, a bitch was extremely sad. My heart felt so empty. It was like Draylon loved everything about me one minute, yet now it's like I've never existed in his life. To make matters worse, he has basically taken my daughter. I know he loves her, and she's okay. However, how can he just do that? It's not right. You just don't stop loving somebody like that. He's hurting me on purpose, and that shit ain't fair. He forcefully took me from my old life and made me fit into his. Now, he's basically removed me from his life. That shit doesn't feel good. I've come to the realization that I love him too much, and he doesn't love me enough.

As I headed home after dinner, I decided to send Draylon a message and be done with it. If our marriage is on the shelf, as he says, then I don't want to be married at all. He thinks I'm weak but I'm about to show him different.

Me: *I've decided that since our marriage is on the shelf. I no longer want to be married at all. My lawyer will be in touch!*

Reluctantly, I pressed send and also took my wedding ring off. I placed it inside of my glove compartment. Once I made it home, I took shit a step further. I packed my shit and got ghost on Draylon and everybody. I just needed some time to relax and be one with myself.

Chapter 10: Latasia

Life as a mom had been nothing short of amazing. Although I'm always talking shit about my fat spoiled baby, I wouldn't change him for anything in the world. God gave me my own little person. I just want to protect Junior from all the evils of the world. Sometimes, I stare at my son as he sleeps and wonder if I will ever fail him. Sometimes, parents fall short with their children and never realize it. All I know is I want to give him the best life ever.

That's why I've been giving Horse nothing but grace these past couple of months. A bitch has been working hard as fuck at exercising self-control. Unfortunately, the nigga Horse loves it when I act a fool. I've promised myself to never be stupid over a nigga again in my life. He and I had a conversation about this bitch Diwanna, and he assured me that there was nothing between them. Still, all of that shit has been a big ass lie. The slick-dick-ass nigga has been meeting up with the whore.

Unbeknownst to Horse, I had linked his phone to mine. Every time he corresponded with that bitch, I've known. At first, it seemed like he was curving her ass. However, two weeks ago, he met up with the bitch for dinner. I didn't say shit. I gave the nigga the benefit of the doubt. A bitch should have known he couldn't keep that demon dick in his pants. It's cool, though. I told this motherfucker not to play with me. Now I'm about to make him wish he never met my ass.

I was sitting inside of my car giving it a little time before I went inside his house. He was currently in there with the bitch, Diwanna. I'm already knowing he's fucking that hoe in 'The Stable'. I knew that after I did what I was about to do, there was no coming back from it. Still, right now, I really don't care. Horse can't keep playing with me. He basically made me fall in love with him and birth a demon seed for him, so I deserve better than for him to be so fucking deceitful. I won't lie and say I'm not hurt because I am, but I'll cry later. Right now, I'm on a mission to fuck some shit up.

When I stepped outside my car, I grabbed the can of gasoline from the trunk. Without making too much noise, I slid inside the patio door. I had come over and unlocked it the day before. I slowly made my way through the house. With each step, I was starting to rethink what I was about to do. A huge lump formed in my throat as I stood in front of the room. Looking at the words *"The Stable"* written on the door angered me. It's funny how the first time I stood in front of this very door, I was very much so afraid. Tears welled up in my eyes at hearing her moaning. I started pouring gasoline all over the door and in front of it. Before setting the shit ablaze, I opened the door. Horse needed to see my face before I killed him and that bitch.

My heart ached, and my anger rose as I observed Horse fucking the shit out of the bitch Diwanna. Her feet and hands were handcuffed, and she was chained up by her neck, with a ball gag in her mouth.

"It ain't nothing between y'all, huh!" I spewed, making my presence known.

"Oh fuckkkk! Tasia!"

"Nah, nigga! Don't Tasia me."

"What the fuck is you doing? Is that gasoline I smell?" Horse started panicking, trying to fix his clothes.

"Yeah, it is. I'll see you and that demon dick in hell!" I seethed, quickly striking a match and dropping it on the floor. The entire door frame engulfed in flames quick as fuck.

I laughed a little, looking at that bitch panicking while she was all chained up shit. I didn't really realize how much gasoline I had poured. The entire door and hallway had gone up in flames. Horse was trying his best to get her out of all the restraints. When I watched him struggling and coughing, I started backing away.

"Tasia! Tasia!" I could hear coughing, struggling, and Horse calling my name. A bitch was too scared to look back, so I hauled ass getting the fuck out of dodge.

| | | | |

Keizon: *Sis, where the fuck you at? I'm worried like a motherfucker.*

La-La*: Bitch, you have lost your mind! If you don't get in contact with somebody, I swear I'm going to beat the hell out of you. We're all worried about you and the baby! Your daddy is alive. Please come home!*

Kateevah: *Here it is I'm on my lying low shit, and your ass is gone in the wind. Wherever your ass at, stay there. Don't answer for nobody. That hoe died in the fire, and Horse barely made it out. I know you didn't mean to snap. I love you. Please let me know if you're good.*

Belladonna: *Now do you see why I say your ass is always in something. Your ass is crazier than I thought. Never in my life did I think you would be a fucking arsonist. Your brother is losing his mind! Please reach out to him. He won't tell anybody. If you don't want to talk to him, call me. You already know I'm not going to say shit. That hoe had it coming! Let somebody know you're okay, crazy bitch!*

The moment I turned my phone on, messages started coming through. Although I was sad and scared as fuck, these motherfuckers had me laughing at them, especially Belladonna. My ass had really fucked-up now. That bitch Diwanna is dead, and Horse is going to be okay. That man's gone fuck me up whenever he gets his hands on me. That's why I'm not responding to anybody, not even Kateevah. Draylon has the power to get her ass to talk. La-La's ass has stooped to a new low, talking about my father is alive. That bitch will say anything to get somebody to do something. Granted, she's my mother and worried, but saying my daddy is alive is downright wrong.

They all thought I was in hiding, but honestly, I wasn't. I never gave up my condo. Although this is where I was shot, it was the only place I felt comfortable outside of the home I shared with Horse. Just thinking of him made me pick my son up and cradle him. Why did he have to go and ruin everything by entertaining that bitch? Then again, why did I have to go and fall in love with him? From the jump, I knew Horse would break my heart, but honestly, I didn't expect it to be so soon. Our son isn't even six months old, but I'm sure we're definitely done. There ain't no way he's going to want me after trying to kill him. It's cool, though, because I don't want to be with that sick-minded-ass-nigga anyway.

Days Later

No Caller ID: *You better bring me my fuckin' son!*

No Caller ID: *You have twenty-four hours!*

No Caller ID: *Bitch, you better hope I don't murder your ass when I get a hold of you. You better bring me my son. This is my last time telling you.*

Horse had been calling me privately and sending threatening messages for days, but I hadn't responded to his ass. The nigga had me scared shitless. At the same time, I wanted to just go home and face him. I needed to get this shit over with so that I could move forward. Junior and I were running out of clothes, and soon, I would have to go get some things, anyway. Plus, I was tired of sitting in this little ass condo.

Living in that big ass house got me spoiled, and I didn't want to live poor anymore. I had been too scared to go out for anything, fearing someone would see me. I'd been getting food and things I needed delivered to me, but I was tired of inconveniencing myself to prove a fucking point. I'm about to take that nigga this baby and get the fuck on gone. I love my son, but I need a fucking vacation. Maybe I'd go wherever the hell it was that Kateevah was hiding out. It was crazy how both of us were going through some shit at the moment and couldn't even be there for each other. We'd let these Prince brothers get the best of us, and the shit was so sad.

My heart rapidly pounded as I stood ringing the doorbell to the house. Clearly, the locks had been changed because my key wasn't working. I bit the bottom of my lip as I switched my son's car seat to my other hand. Junior was heavy as fuck. The moment I was getting ready to walk back to my car, the door opened.

"Oh my god, get in here! We've been worried crazy!" Annalise practically yanked the car seat from me.

"I'm fine. I just came to get us some clothes."

"No. You have to get the hell out of here before Horse comes back. Please, Tasia! I'm begging you. I'll tell him you called me, and I went to pick the baby up."

"I'm not leaving without getting some of my shit."

"I do not want him to put his hands on you, Latasia!"

"If that nigga put his hands on me, we're going to rumble in this bitch!"

"Did you forget you tried to kill him because he hasn't? That damn girl died in that fire, and now her people want answers. I'm telling you, Tasia. Please get the hell out of here before he comes back."

"I appreciate the warning, Annalise. However, I'm not going anywhere. It's his fault that bitch is dead! Had he not been out cheating on me with that bitch none of this shit would have happened. He lied to me. I distinctly told his ass not to play with me, but the nigga thought the shit was a game. I showed him I'm nothing to play with. As a matter of fact, I'm going to wait for his ass to come back."

Annalise was really looking scared. I won't front like I'm not afraid, but a bitch was not about to be running. It would only be a matter of time before Horse was snatching my ass up anyway, so I might as well get this shit over with.

"Well gone 'head with your big bad ass. I'm taking my grandson with me. You and Horse are nuts, and Junior is not about to be around this craziness. Call me if you need me."

I was happy as hell when Annalise said she was going to take Junior with her. The last thing I wanted was to be going back and forth with his stupid ass daddy. Although I was going to wait for Horse to come home, I still decided to pack some things. No matter what happened, I knew we were over. Honestly, I was ready to start the healing process.

After packing, I nervously sat around, waiting for him to arrive. All that courage I had a minute ago had subsided. My decision to stay had changed. A bitch was about to get the fuck out of dodge. I grabbed the bag and some money out of the safe before running down the stairs to leave out. The moment I opened the door, Horse, Draylon, and the sneaky bitch Nautica were stepping inside.

"I see I'm about to start another fire! My friend leaves, and now you with this bitch!" For a couple of seconds, I forgot about my issue with Horse. This nigga Draylon was with this hoe, and I know for a fact Kateevah doesn't know. I don't play about my bitch, so we can all definitely scrap.

"Let me holla at you for a second!" Before I could react, Horse grabbed me by my long ass ponytail and basically walked my ass right back up the stairs.

"Chill, bro!" I heard Draylon yell, but Horse ignored his ass.

"Nigga, you better let my hair go!" I screamed. The nigga was pulling my hair so hard tears were filling up my eyes.

Before I knew it, Horse had picked me up and slammed me hard as fuck on the floor. He picked my big ass up like he was the Incredible Hulk.

"Shut the fuck up! Where the fuck is my son?" I managed to look up and see him standing over me with his gun out.

"Your momma took him home with her." My entire body hurt just trying to answer the question. I'm positive this nigga done broke something.

"Good! Get the fuck up, and if you take too long. I'm going to body slam your ass again. Clearly, you don't know who the fuck I am."

"I definitely don't!" I mumbled under my breath.

"What the fuck did you just say? Speak up! Get your bitch ass up!"

The moment Horse yanked me up, I started swinging. It was like all the pain had subsided. We were fighting all over the room and breaking shit. I was windmilling the fuck out of him. The sound of gunshots and seeing the flame from the gun made me drop down to my knees.

"Ahhhhh! Why the fuck is you shooting?" This nigga was shooting inside of the bedroom like he was crazy. All I saw was flashbacks of Rico shooting me. I was crying, shaking, and had pissed all over myself.

"Horse! What the fuck, bro? Please tell me you didn't kill Tasia!" Draylon yelled through the bedroom door while he beat on it.

"Nah, her pissy ass is still alive!" He laughed as he pulled a blunt from behind his ear.

"Open the door and let me see for myself. Nigga, you tripping!" Draylon demanded.

"Nah, I'm not opening the door. Tell my brother you're good!" Horse gritted while pointing the gun at me.

"I'm okay, Draylon. I loudly declared, trying to sound as strong as possible.

"Okay, but open the door, bro. We have to go handle that thing!" Draylon instructed.

I closed my eyes tight and silently prayed he would leave.

"Give me a minute. I promise I'm good. Stand the fuck up!"

As I stood to my feet, I couldn't believe I had pissed everywhere.

"You proved your point, Dayvion. Just let me leave!" I hated I was standing in front of him looking so damn sad and pitiful. The look on his face let me know he was enjoying seeing me weak.

"Let you leave! We locked the fuck in! You're not going no motherfucking where! The only reason I haven't murdered you and tossed your fucking body in the Chicago River is because I love you, and I don't want my son growing up without his momma. Plus, I was in the wrong. Had I not been with the bitch Diwanna, we wouldn't even be right here. I just let them shots off to show you what the fuck it's like for the person you love to try to kill you.

Yeah, you caught me fucking that bitch, but at the same time, you could have killed me, Tasia! Do you think I want to get married to a woman who can't control her emotions? Well, I don't. That hasty decision you made almost killed me and made me lose my fucking freedom. You didn't think of the repercussions, Latasia, and that's a fucking problem for me! You know the fucking life I lead. I would have rather you leave a nigga than try to kill me.

Do you know how badly I really want to kill you?" Horse angrily tapped the gun up against his head.

Yeah, this nigga was out of his fucking mind.

"Why don't you just do it then? Kill me, Dayvion! Since you want to so bad!" I challenged.

"Nah, I love you too much to do that. Plus, you're no good to me dead! Get comfortable because it's going to be a long fucking time before you see the outside of this house! As of right now, you're my prisoner! Get cleaned up. I'll be back shortly. Do not try to leave this fucking house. Go wash your pissy ass up, acting like you're scared of a nigga. Your big bad tough ass is not scared of me. You tried to kill me, Latasia, and I'm hurt," Horse admitted.

I wanted to laugh so badly, but I was so scared he would start shooting again.

Once Horse left out of the room, I quickly breathed a sigh of relief. The sound of him locking the house down made me jump. I rushed to the window and observed him. This nigga was really serious about me being his prisoner. My dumb ass should have listened when Annalise told me to hurry and leave. A bitch didn't come over here with the intention of becoming this nigga's prisoner. Honestly, I thought Horse was going to beat the fuck out of me, not put me on my shit one good time, and slightly rough me the fuck up. He had me confused as hell.

After gathering my thoughts, I took a long hot bath. I'm sure my body was going to be sore like a motherfucker. I'm still in shock behind Horse body slamming my ass. Like, why would his crazy ass do me like that? Kateevah crossed my mind, so I grabbed my phone to FaceTime her.

"I was wondering when your ass was going to call. Are you okay?" Kateevah asked as soon as the call connected.

"I'm good for now. I guess. Horse has me locked in the house. His crazy ass was shooting inside of the bedroom and everything. It scared the fuck out of me. All I could think about was when Rico shot me. What if he really shoots me? He says that he wants to kill me so bad." I stated.

"Stop crying, Tasia. That nutty nigga is not going to kill you. Horse

loves your crazy ass. Plus, if he was going to kill you. Your ass would be dead, and you know it. If anything, he's mad because they have to clean up that situation your ass caused. For the record, you didn't do anything wrong. The bitch had it coming," Kateevah assured me.

"Speaking of bitches that got it coming, today Draylon and Horse came to the house, and the bitch Nautica was with them. I definitely said something to Draylon's ass about it. Have you talked to him?" I asked, spilling all the tea to my best friend.

"No. We honestly don't communicate if it's not about Unique. I guess it is for me to come to grips with the current state of our relationship. That's why I had to get away. I thought coming out here to Vegas would lift my spirits. Honestly, the shit has made me sadder. I wish you could come out here."

"Don't cry. I'm coming out there. Just give me like two days," I assured her.

"How are you going to do that? Horse is not about to let you out of the house. I'm going to just come home. Being here won't change the reality of my situation. I'd rather be there with people instead of out here alone," Kateevah stated.

"No, you need this time, and I do, too. I'm going to figure out a way to smooth shit out with Horse. I know what I have to do. Look at us crying and feeling all fucked-up about things. It seems like just a minute ago, shit was normal for us. Let me ask you something. Do you regret running into Draylon?" I quizzed.

"As much as I want to regret it. I can't. If there is nothing else, I know. It's that I love that man. Being married to him has been the best thing ever. Draylon would kill the world for Unique and me. He thinks I ain't loyal to him. Right now, he's not seeing how fucking much I love him. It's cool, though. God knows my heart, and that's all that matters. I'm not kissing his ass for us to be together. As far as Nautica goes, Annalise told me they found out where their son was. I'm happy for Draylon, but I'm focusing on myself. I love him too much, and I don't like how that makes me feel. Look, let me get off this phone before I be ugly crying. If you don't come, within the next couple of days of coming home. Belladonna has been calling and cussing me out every day. She's been talking about you and me like a dog," Kateevah informed me.

"I'm going to call her and let her know I'm okay. She and Keizon have been worried like shit. I'll reach out to them tomorrow. Right now, I just want to relax and get some rest before Horse comes back. That nigga picked me up and body slammed my ass. I just knew he was going to turn my ass every which way but loose. Hell, I think he ain't done with my ass. I have a plan, though, friend. Get ready because I'm coming to Vegas. I love you, friend."

"I love you too."

After hanging up with Kateevah, I continued to soak in the tub. My mind was in deep thought about how to smooth this shit out with Horse. He's right. I should have thought about the repercussions. I didn't think I could go to jail for it. Hell, I wasn't even thinking about my freedom. Jealousy and hurt consumed me. Now, don't get it twisted. I'm not really sorry I did it, nor am I sorry that hoe perished. She shouldn't have been fucking my man, and he definitely shouldn't have been fucking her. However, I'll fake it until I make it. In order to get Horse off my ass and let me go to Vegas, I need to apologize for some shit that I'm not sorry for. I wish that would suffice, but I know it won't. A bitch is gone have to let him dominate me in the worse way. I'm sure that would satisfy him. It's obvious that's what he loves to use as a form of punishment. Instead of him killing me, I would rather him hurt me sexually.

Chapter 11: Horse

I had more shit on my plate than a little bit. Draylon was pulling me in all different directions when I had my own bullshit to deal with this whole time. I can't believe Tasia set my fucking stable on fire. I'm madder than a motherfucker. That shit wasn't supposed to go down that way. I never had any intention of fucking Diwanna. The shit just happened. The bitch paid me fifty thousand dollars to be dominated, and there was no way I was turning it down. The moment she wired the funds to my account, I sent them to Latasia's account. She's an ungrateful ass heifer, not to mention crazier than a motherfucker. I told her ass I was hurt, but a nigga's really scared of her ass. She damn near burnt my entire fucking crib down. Her ass is lucky I have an external state-of-the-art fire extinguishing system. Unfortunately, for Diwanna, there wasn't a system inside the room because it was an add-on after the house was built. Luckily, I had a hidden door that led to my office. Had I not been able to escape there, I would be dead too.

I really wanted to murder Tasia's ass. Had she been anybody else, her whole family would be dead. I promised my nigga Keizon I wouldn't kill her. However, I made sure to let him know I wasn't letting her ass off easily. Regardless of how I feel about what she did, I have to take this one on the chin and handle it in a way I'm not used to. I saw the hurt in her eyes, which was the last thing I wanted to do, so I needed to take it easy on her. At the same time, she needed to know not to fuck with me.

"What the fuck happened to you niggas?" Hearing Nautica's irritating ass voice brought me out of my thoughts. We were all in the Tahoe headed to an address we found going through the paperwork.

"Shut the fuck up!" I gritted.

"No, I'm serious. I know all of our lives have changed. However, I never thought I would witness you niggas emotional over bitches. Not you two heartless, heartbreaking motherfuckers. This shit is hilarious."

"What the fuck is so funny?"

"Y'all being in love with them big bitches!"

"Laugh all you want, but I'll choose Kateevah over you any day! Fuck you mean? She's a bad bitch, and you know it! Fuck out of here!"

"You know Latasia's putting bitches to shame, including you. Not too much with the disrespect. They're both dying to lay hands on you!"

"Whatever! Let's just get over to this address. I hope and pray Junior is there. I'm going to get my son, and none of y'all have to ever be worried about me. I'm not sure who the Prince family is anymore. Everything is so weird. I wish Draya were here."

"Why so y'all could be sucking on each other pussy like her and Shameeka was?" Draylon stated, and I fell out laughing. Bro was wild as fuck for saying that.

"What? I don't know what the fuck you are talking about. Draya and I have never crossed that fucking line. That was my best friend and my sister. She and Shameeka weren't fucking around either. Draya was not gay. My girl kept her a roster. The only reason y'all didn't know is because she knew you all would give the man a hard ass time. As far as the bitch Shameeka goes, she wasn't fucking your sister. She was fucking your father. Annalise walked in on them having sex. She was pissy drunk when saw caught them. She was still drunk as hell when she told Draya what she saw. In order to keep the peace, Draya convinced your momma that she saw her and Shameeka having sex, not your father." she countered.

"Fuck out of here with that bullshit, Nautica!" I yelled and turned around to look at her sitting in the back seat.

"I'm telling you what Draya told me the last time she visited. I've been in jail the whole time. How would I know anything about what was going on?" Nautica pointed out.

I looked over at my brother and saw that his jaw was twitching. My blood was boiling listening to her say this fuck shit. Just when you think shit can't get any worse.

"Why the fuck are you telling us this shit now? When you came by the office, you could have revealed this shit too."

"Listen to me, Draylon. I don't stand to gain anything by hurting y'all. Why would I ever want to do that? Do you actually think I wanted to tell you your wife was fucking your father? That's a different type of hurt. Honestly, I don't want it to be true, but I know it is. Draya never cries, and she was brokenhearted about everything that was transpiring behind y'all back. I'm not sure what Mr. Prince was holding over her head, but it had to be something big for her to sit at a table and vote you out. Even I know she had a loyalty to her brothers that was unmatched. Draya didn't mean for things to go down the way that it did."

"Fuck Draya! Stop speaking so fucking highly of her ass. She basically gave your fucking kid away. You're defending a scandalous ass bitch. Just shut the fuck up and sit back. We don't want to hear any more fucking revelations!" I had to go off so she could just stop talking.

This was like another dagger, not to mention more confusion about Draya's motives. Like why in the fuck would you play a mind game with your mother? All I can think is if Annalise really did know and played along with it. One thing about Annalise is she ain't ever been no dummy. She's a real thorough ass female. She just got lost inside of a bottle fucking with a nigga like our pops. Draylon was quiet as fuck. I wanted to say something to him, but now wasn't the time. There was no way we could talk freely in front of this snake-ass bitch. I'm positive we're going to have to murk her ass. She knows too much and talks too much.

For the rest of the ride, we were all quiet. I was more than ready to get this shit over and get back to the crib to talk to Tasia. Hopefully, the urge to whoop her ass doesn't consume me.

"This is the address. When we get up to the door, let me do the talking, Nautica!"

"Why can't I say shit? That's my son too!"

"I don't give a fuck! You heard what the fuck I said!" Draylon gritted.

I can't wait until he smacks the fuck out of her. She doesn't listen at all. Now that I remember, the bitch never did listen. That's how her ass ended up in jail. Not fucking listening.

"As a matter of fact, stay your ass in the car!" I yelled, and we hopped out and quickly locked her ass inside. Nautica couldn't get out unless we unlocked the doors.

We both grabbed our Glocks and walked up to the house. Nautica was acting a fool in the truck, but we ignored her ass.

"I can't believe we all the way out here in fucking Winnetka. Who the fuck does Draya know out here?" I ranted.

"Ain't no telling. Let's just see what we can find out and get back to the city. I'm not feeling none of this shit, lil bro. Nautica's not making the situation better. I really want to put a bullet in her fucking head, but I can't move hasty. I'm sure the bitch knows some more secrets, and I need to know everything that she knows."

"I agree. Let's see what's to these motherfuckers!"

We made it up to the door and started banging on the door. A couple of seconds passed, and the door opened. Draylon and I looked at each other, then down at the kid. It didn't take a rocket scientist to see that this was indeed my brother's son.

"What did I tell you about opening the door, DJ?" A beautiful Spanish woman appeared behind him.

"I thought it was Aunt Draya." He sounded sad and walked away from the door. That stung a little. He was clearly waiting for Draya to come back, which proved she had been in his life. At least the bitch didn't just give him to strangers.

"I'm sorry. Can I help you guys with anything?"

"Yes. I got this address from my sister, Draya. She's in jail, and she wanted us to come over and pick up DJ."

"She never told me she had brothers. I've actually been trying to find someone who was related. He's been here for months waiting for her to return. She asked me to keep an eye on him, but she never returned. I'm Letecia. Please come inside."

She stepped to the side and allowed us to enter. DJ was sitting on the sofa, scrolling on his phone.

"I know who you are." he declared in a low tone while looking at Draylon.

"Who am I?"

"You're my dad. My aunt Draya talked about you all the time and showed me pictures. Are you here to take me home? She told me if you ever showed up, then I have to go with you."

For the first time in my life, I watched my brother get choked up in front of others. He kneeled in front of DJ and stared at him.

"Yeah. I'm here to take you home, son." It was a beautiful sight seeing them embrace.

"Thanks for keeping an eye on him for us. Please give me your banking information. My family would like to compensate you for your troubles."

"Absolutely not. I've been babysitting DJ since he was a baby. You might as well say he's, my godson. I'll never take monetary gifts for helping out with his care. Draya has always been such a good provider for him. I knew about his mom being in jail, but Draya never spoke about her family."

"We were under the impression that she had put him up for adoption. That's how we found this address. It was on some paperwork."

"Yes, this is my home, and I told her she could use this address if she needed to. I'm not sure why you all thought she had given him up for adoption. Draya has had him ever since he was about a month old. Listen, I'm so happy that you guys showed up. DJ has been really sad waiting for her to show up. I knew it had to be something serious since she hadn't reached out. For a minute, I thought she was dead."

"If you don't mind me asking, how did you and Draya come to know each other? I'm asking because we've never heard anything about you. Clearly, she trusted you if she left DJ in your care," I inquired.

"When I first came here, I was an illegal immigrant. I needed a job, and she had placed an ad stating that she needed a live-in nanny. That's how we met. Draya helped me to get my citizenship. She purchased me this house and helped me live a good life here in the States. Draya has been a really great friend. DJ, go grab some of your things so you can go with your dad." Letecia instructed.

"Please let me give you some money. I appreciate you holding him down in our absence. I just recently learned about his existence. Honestly, I never in a million years thought I would come here and see him in the flesh. I'm indebted to you forever," Draylon expressed.

DJ came back out carrying his book bag and a basketball in his arm. Just looking at him made me anxious to see what my son would look like at this age.

"Again, I don't want anything for taking care of him. Just make sure I can call and check on him every now and then. Here... these are his vital documents and shot records. I've always had a copy in the event I needed them. I love you, DJ. Be good. Remember to keep reading a book a week. I'm going to be checking in with your dad and uncle to make sure. Give me so dap." They dapped it up, and she hugged him tight. After giving them some time to say goodbye, we headed back out to the truck.

"There is somebody inside of the truck I want you to meet. Don't be afraid if she's crying. They'll be happy tears because she has waited a long time to see you." Draylon grabbed his son's hand, and they walked ahead of me.

I fell back and allowed them some time before getting in the truck. Thoughts of Draya consumed me. She and I were close as fuck. We were literally together for hours, day in and day out, which is why I simply can't understand how I never noticed anything different about her. I wished this shit would have come out before Draylon took her out. Maybe we could get a better understanding. Unfortunately, we will never get the closure we need from that situation. All we can do is continue living, eliminating all threats, and taking our family to new heights.

Hours Later

I had been sitting inside my man cave for hours, getting

fucked up. Tasia was still locked inside our bedroom. I had yet to go up and check on her. A nigga felt like he needed to get drunk as fuck so I could just pass out. After the shit that transpired between us earlier, I'm sure she doesn't want to see my ass. Honestly, I feel ashamed to look at her. I went too far shooting off that gun in the room with her. That quick, I let my anger get the best of me. I forgot not too long ago that Tasia was shot and traumatized behind. It was only recently I realized she was finally sleeping through the night. I'm sure I've set her progress back tremendously. Although I'm still pissed the fuck off with Tasia, I'm happy I know the whereabouts of her and my son. When she was hiding from me, I was about to lose my mind.

As I sit knocking back shots of Don Julio and smoking a fat ass blunt. I can't help but wonder if I should just co-parent with Tasia. Maybe our love is too toxic to continue. We haven't been together long, yet we fight like an old married couple. The shit is not healthy. Letting that gun off the way that I did let me know I'm way past gone over Tasia. She has me acting out of character, and I don't like the shit at all.

Reluctantly, I stood to my feet and headed up to our bedroom. A nigga was feeling no pain, so I felt like I could just go to sleep. Then again, I probably shouldn't be trying to sleep next to her crazy ass. What if she tries to kill my ass in my sleep? This time, she might be successful.

After entering the code in the panel, the door opened for me. The lights cut on the moment I stepped inside. Tasia was sleeping with her back up against the headboard.

"Tasia!"

"Huh?"

Hearing me call her name made her jump. The fear in her eyes and her body language fucked me up. I removed my clothes and climbed into bed next to her. The room was spinning, so I laid on my back.

"You can leave. I'm not going to force you to stay. Just don't take my son away from me and pull a disappearing act. There are plenty of properties you can live on. I'll stay out of your way. Just allow me to be a father. All I want to do is co-parent. Do you think you could do that?"

"Okay." Her head was now hanging low.

"I'm sorry for earlier. I never should have fired that gun. That was fucked up on my part. I know you've struggled mentally behind being shot. I was dead ass wrong."

"It's cool. I'm sorry for trying to kill you. I just lost my mind when I saw you having sex with her. I wasn't thinking clearly. You were right. I let my emotions get the best of me, and it could have cost us our freedom. In that moment, I didn't think about our son, and he is who matters the most. I'll leave in the morning."

My eyes were closed, but I felt Tasia get out of the bed.

"Where are you going?"

"To the bathroom."

After a couple of seconds passed, I heard the water cut on, but it didn't drown out the sound of her crying. Hearing Tasia break down made me quickly rush into the bathroom. She was sitting on the floor, bawling. I sat next to her and wrapped my arms around her.

"Tasia. Come on, baby! Please don't cry."

"All night, I've been practicing what I would say to you. I didn't think you were going to come home and say let's co-parent. Honestly, I knew you weren't going to want me after what I did. It's just the reality of us breaking up hit me hard, but I'll be okay." She wiped her face and winced as she got up from the floor.

Seeing her leaning over the bathroom sink really fucked me up.

"Are you in pain?"

"What do you think, Horse? You body slammed me on the hard ass marble floor, but I'll be okay."

"I'm sorry, Tasia. Just come lay back down. Do you want me to get you anything?"

"Nah, I'm good." She walked past me and slowly climbed back into bed.

When I climbed into bed next to Tasia, she turned her back to me, but I wrapped my arm around her anyway. I regretted telling her we should co-parent. I no longer heard crying, but I felt the sadness radiating off her. The effects of the tequila and weed finally put me to sleep.

| | | | |

The next morning, I woke up to find Tasia no longer in bed with me. I needed to take a leak, so I rushed to the bathroom. Before I could reach the toilet, The mirror on the wall caught my eye. It was a message written in red lipstick that read.

REAL BITCHES DON'T CRY. THEY GO TO VEGAS XOXOXO!!

I should have known all that crying shit was cap. Tasia tricked the fuck out of me. All I can do is laugh to keep from catching a flight and strangling her ass.

Chapter 12: Belladonna

It's been a minute since I wanted to lay hands on my daughter. Her ass better hope that I've calmed down by the time we see each other. One thing I've never played about is my grandbaby, and Kateevah knows that. She needs to bring her ass home and be a mother. I don't care how brokenhearted I was behind Kato. Leaving my daughter because I needed some 'me time' wasn't the move.

I don't know what's wrong with this younger generation of mothers talking about how they need vacations away from their children. Every time I felt like I needed to get away, my child came with me. This is unacceptable, and I'm very disappointed in Kateevah.

I regretted being supportive of her allowing Draylon into their life. He came in and turned her upside down mentally. My baby is sad, and I hate that for her. Meanwhile, Unique is happy and living her best life. All she sees is this new spoiled-ass life with her daddy. She's too young to understand that her mother is going through it. I'm glad about that. However, Kateevah had better bring her ass home before Unique starts feeling abandoned.

I know I might be exaggerating, but I'm concerned about my daughter. I've been so caught up with my own relationship that I've slacked in mothering. Kateevah and I have always been the best of friends, but I always made sure to remind her I'm still her mother. Since we all got hooked up with these niggas, we've lost sight of what the fuck is important — us as women and who the fuck we are.

Tasia has lost her fucking mind, too. Her ass is around here setting fires and killing bitches. I'm glad Keizon doesn't carry the last name Prince. Horse and Draylon got Latasia and Kateevah all types of fucked up. Both of them heifers are in Vegas having the time of their lives. Any other time, I would agree with them having me time. However, it's time for them to come home and deal with their issues head-on. Draylon loves Kateevah. He's just in his feelings. Deep down inside, that man knows my daughter loves him. I'm minding my business, but I'll stand on business when it comes down to what the fuck I birthed. Draylon had better get his shit together. He promised me that he wouldn't hurt my baby. Right now, he's so mad at her that he doesn't see how hurt she is.

As I sit across from my grandbaby eating breakfast, I can't help but stare at her. Kateevah did a really good job at raising her alone for the first six years of her life. However, now that Unique has been with her dad and his family. It's like Kateevah doesn't exist. Unique hasn't asked about her momma once. I might be overthinking it, but it doesn't feel right.

"Grandma, I have a brother. His name is DJ."

"I heard. How does it feel having a big brother?"

"It's so much fun. My daddy lets us eat all the junk food we want, and he lets us stay up all night watching movies."

"Wow. I bet that's a lot of fun. I can't wait to meet your brother. Come on. Hurry and eat so Moe can get you to school on time. He's outside waiting. Do you want to call your momma?" I grabbed my phone and started dialing Kateevah's number.

"No. Mommy always cries, and it makes me sad, grandma. She moved away because my daddy made her heartbroken.

"No. Your momma didn't move away. She just needed to go on a vacation for a little while. Come on. Let's go."

Hearing my granddaughter say all of that angered me. She's too young to be knowing grown people's business. That was all I needed to hear. I'm taking my ass to Vegas and bring Kateevah's ass home. This shit is bigger than Draylon. Her daughter is watching her behavior, and it's not okay.

Once I got Unique out of the door and off to school, I rushed upstairs to my bedroom to pack. Keizon was still asleep, drunk from the night before. Ever since he found out his father was still alive; he has been in a dark place. Honestly, I need a break from his motherfucking ass, too.

"Where the fuck are you going, Belladonna?"

"To Vegas!"

I kept walking around the room, packing my shit. Keizon was now sitting up in bed smoking on a blunt, looking at me like he was in his feelings, which I didn't care about. My only concern was getting to my daughter.

"You're just going to go to Vegas without discussing the shit with me first?"

"When it comes down to Kateevah, I don't have to discuss shit with anyone. Listen, my daughter and your sister need me right now, so I'm not trying to be a bitch toward you. Right now, I need to be a parent. I promise I'll be back in two days." I was now standing over the bed, stroking his beard.

"I hear you, baby. Come ride this dick before you take flight." Keizon removed the cover from his body, and his dick was standing tall as the Eiffel Tower.

My mouth salivated, looking at all that hard ass chocolate. A bitch didn't hesitate coming up out of my clothes. I'll just have to catch a later flight. Right now, I needed to calm the beast down. My husband was extremely needy, so he definitely wasn't feeling me going to Vegas, but at the same time, he knew I needed to go check on them.

Latasia still hadn't reached out to him, so that was another thing that was hurting him. Keizon was alone, and it pissed me off that his family was all losing their fucking minds. La-La hasn't even been around since that nigga came back from the grave. I'm already knowing I'm going to beat her ass again about playing with my husband's feelings. I'm about to do this dick, and then I'm catching a flight out to bring Dumb and Dumber home. I'm standing on fucking business and getting this family back on track.

Las Vegas: Ceaser's Palace

"What are you doing here, ma?" The shock on Kateevah's face

was priceless. I pushed right past her ass and went inside of her penthouse suite.

"I came to take you and that pyromaniac home. Where's she at?"

"She's in the back sleep. Why you didn't call before you came?"

"I don't have to call your ass to tell you I'm coming, especially when you didn't give me a fucking courtesy call letting me know you were leaving the fucking city. Now, I've kept my mouth shut and stayed out of your marriage—"

"I don't have a marriage."

"Don't cut me off, Kateevah!"

"It's true, ma! I'm no longer married. Draylon put our marriage on the shelf, so that's where the fuck I'm going to leave it. Like I said, I'm no longer married."

"Sit the fuck down... right now! I've been behaving like your friend for too fucking long, so long that you've forgotten I'm your mother! Don't ever disrespect me like that again, Kateevah! I know you are a grown woman with a child of your own. However, you are still my child."

"I'm sorry, ma." Kateevah had finally sat the fuck down, which I was happy because if I had to tell her again, I was definitely going to beat her ass.

"What are you doing out here, Belladonna?" Tasia asked, looking a hot ass mess.

"I came out here to take y'all back home. Playtime is over. Y'all done had your fun and proved a point. It's time to go home and get your fucking kids."

"I'm not ready to go home. Horse is doing just fine without me. That man said he would rather co-parent, so now he is the parent!" Tasia protested.

Now she doesn't sound like a damn fool.

"Unique loves being with Draylon. I'm positive she's okay with me. I'll go home in a couple of weeks. Plus, this vacation is on him. I'm not done spending his money," Kateevah chimed in.

For a couple of seconds, I sat looking at both of them, all the while wondering where in the fuck did I go wrong.

"Listen, both of y'all going about this shit the wrong way. One thing a woman should never do is pull a disappearing act on her children. You're not punishing them niggas. They make enough money to pay fucking babysitters, not to mention Annalise and I have had your fucking kids more than anything, which neither of us are complaining. However, you need to put proving a point to Horse and Draylon on the back burner. Your focus should be on your kids," I advised. "Kateevah, have you ever known me to leave you when I'm going through something with a nigga? Answer that for me?"

"No, I was always with you."

"Exactly! Because no matter what the fuck I go through in this life or with a motherfucking nigga, my child comes first! Do you know Unique doesn't want to talk on the phone with you because you're sad? Not only that, but she is getting very fond of her brother, which means his sneaky pussy ass mother is around Draylon. Are you really about to just fall back and not fight for your marriage? You're not married to a regular nigga, Kateevah! He's got old long ass money! If you keep laying your ass around this penthouse, you're not going to be able to come home to that Prince luxury that is now yours. That bitch wants your spot! I'm going to let you sit and think on what I just said."

I took a second to gather my thoughts before speaking again.

"Tasia, you know we've always had a love/hate relationship. However, we have become closer since I married your brother. Your relationship with Kateevah has always made me fuss at you like you were a daughter, too. I know La-La doesn't have a clue how to be a parent if money isn't involved. However, I love you enough to let you know that leaving your infant son is not the move. He's a baby, and he needs his mother. Yes, Horse hurt you, but that doesn't mean you hurt the baby. Do you know that if Horse hadn't got out of that fire, your son would be an orphan? His father would be dead, and his mother would be in jail for the rest of her life. I know you were crazy as fuck, but I didn't think you were this fucking unhinged. You are lucky that man didn't kill you. The mother in me has to tell you that. The woman in me is here to let you know you did what you had to do. However, in the future, think about your child first. That goes for the both of you."

"I'll go home tomorrow. I'm not kissing Draylon's ass, though." Kateevah got up and walked off.

I knew she was mad, but I came out here and got on her ass. She was not fooling me one bit. Her ass was going home because of that bitch Nautica. I knew exactly what to say to light some fire under that big-ass booty of hers.

"What about you, pyromaniac? Your brother is really upset with you. Why haven't you answered his calls or texts? He has been worried sick. You, of all people, know how overprotective Keizon is," I reminded her.

"I know. Honestly, I have not reached out because I do not want it to be drama. This is not one of those relationships where my brother can just show up and whoop a nigga's ass behind me. Even though I know his loyalty will always be with me, the business he has with Draylon and Horse is extremely lucrative for him. I will not get in the way of the good life Keizon is living. I'll talk to him as soon as the flight lands. I promise."

"What about Horse?"

"What about him? I'm only going back because of my son. One thing is for sure, and two for certain: I am not a bad mother. Thanks, Belladonna. We both needed this talk."

I was surprised when Tasia hugged me. It felt good to get them to understand where I was coming from. Tasia can cut the bullshit. She knows she loves that weird ass nigga Horse. They are both made for each other because no one out here will want to deal with either of them.

As I sat relaxing on the comfortable sofa. A text came through from Keizon.

Husband: *Do not tell my sister about Lynwood. I have decided not to tell her anything. Do not worry. I got it all figured out. I love you, baby. Hurry back home and do that thing with your mouth that I like.*

I blushed at that last comment. That man loves the way I suck that dick, which is why he be acting a damn fool behind me.

Me: *You have my word that I will not say anything. I love you, too. We will be home tomorrow night.*

I'm not sure what it is, but from the jump, Keizon has been skeptical since learning his father was alive. La-La's ass acted like she cared about Tasia being gone, but that only lasted for one day because the moment that nigga Lynwood called her, she left our house and had not been back. That's another reason why I just want to whoop her ass. She is a piss poor ass mother. I don't give a fuck how old your kid gets. They will always need you. La-La's ass is never around when they really need her. If they are not offering money, the bitch doesn't want no parts.

As I sat thinking of Keizon, I wondered what he meant by he has it all figured out.

Chapter 13: Keizon

From the moment my father popped back up, I had been on a mission to get down to the bottom of what the fuck he had going on. At first, I thought I could put my ear to the streets by talking to some old heads, but none of them really knew anything about the infamous Lynwood Kirkland. The niggas he came up with were dead or in jail. Since I couldn't find any information on my own, it was time I went straight to the source. My father needed to tell me every fucking thing I needed to know.

I had not been able to shake the feeling that it was some bullshit in the game. The thing about drinking and smoking is it makes you think, especially if you're thinking motherfucker who knows how to read people. Luckily for me, I have mastered that shit. The moment he mentioned something about the Prince family, I knew something wasn't right. He's been alive all this time yet never showed his face once. Now, all of a sudden, he's alive and well. It's no coincidence that he magically appeared after she sold that raggedy ass house. How in the fuck did Lynwood know anything about our dealings? Either La-La told him, or he had been watching us in the shadows for the longest time.

Either way, he got me fucked up. There is no way I'm going to let him or La-La fuck our life. It's clear they will always be out for themselves. That's why I don't want my sister to know that he's alive. It will hurt the fuck out of her. She took his death hard. Honestly, I did too. Life when Lynwood was alive was the best. When he died, the good life died too. That's why I'm so angry with La-La. I know for a fact she didn't know he was alive all this time. Had she known, she would have lived her life instead of sitting in that raggedy ass house wasting away. Don't get me wrong. I want nothing more than for my father to truly be here with the best intentions, but the reality is that he's not. I'm not sure if La-La is aware or if she's too in love to see his true face.

| | | | |

La-La's House

"Thanks for coming over. I know you were under the impression your mother was going to be here, but honestly, I thought it would be better if she were not. I feel like, in my absence, you were the man of the house, so it's only right we have a conversation man to man."

"Let's get to the conversation. I need to go pick up my wife from the airport." I nonchalantly stated because I had removed my emotions from the situation Prior to stepping inside the house.

I'm happy La-La wasn't here. The last time she was at my crib, she was acting differently.

"I'm sorry that you all had to grow up thinking that I was dead, but that's the way the government intended it to be. You see, back in the day, I trafficked for the Prince family. What I did not know was that the FEDs were closing in on Drayton. The plan was for him to fly out with the dope on a private plane to Texas. However, at the last minute, he sent me in his place. The moment I landed at the private airstrip, FEDs surrounded me. They were disappointed that it was me and not him. It was never really about trafficking. They wanted to take Drayton and his family down. At first, I refused to take a deal, but that shit changed when I overheard the nigga laughing about setting me up to take the fall. To make matters worse, the nigga put a hit out on me. I went to shower, and that's when I was damn near stabbed to death. The moment I woke up from the coma, I decided to turn against they snake asses. That's why you need to stop fucking with them motherfuckers. Neither you nor your sister are safe."

"You still a lying son of a bitch, Lynwood."

Hearing La-La's voice, I turned around to see her pointing a gun at him. "Ma! What the fuck is you doing?"

"I'm doing what the fuck I should have done the first day he showed up."

"La-La, this is me baby! We discussed this. Why the fuck would you come here? You know I'm trying to save our fucking kids! Put the fucking gun down, and we can talk." my father instructed.

"I'm not putting shit down! You know, from the moment your lying ass showed up, I had a bad feeling. Call it a woman's intuition. Each and every time you touched me, I became disgusted with your ass! Nigga, quit moving before I shoot your ass!" she seethed.

My eyes bucked, looking at La-La pop her shit. I was about to try to stop her, but I decided to fall back and let her work.

"Baby, put the gun down."

"Nah! You see, all of this time, I've been here alone like a damn fool, waiting for you to come home. Deep down inside, I always knew your ass was not dead, so I sat in that fucking house day in and day out because I wanted to be there when you came home. You knew all I had in this world was you. I had no family. It was me, you, and our kids. You promised me a life and pulled a disappearing act on my ass! Nigga, you've been lurking in the shadows, watching us suffer without you. I neglected my children and became a fucking hermit! Not only that, but your ass is lying about the Prince family. You never worked with Drayton or for his family. If my memory serves me right, you were in your feelings because Drayton never fucked with you. The moment you said what you said to Keizon that day he caught us, I knew you were lying. So, I waited until you went to sleep and went through that phone. Nigga, you have a whole other family!" La-La shot him in the stomach, and he went down like a ton of bricks.

I couldn't fucking believe what I was witnessing.

"Ahhhhhh! Sonnn!" He reached out for my leg, but I knocked his hand off of me.

"You aren't here to save our kids. You're here to take from them. The moment you got wind of them having ties with the Prince family. You magically came back from the dead. You're here working against your own kids. We suffered for too long without you. There is no way I'll allow my children to suffer in your presence!" La-La spewed before firing the gun again.

I jumped back the moment his brains splattered on the floor

beneath him.

La-La had shot him right in the temple. She was shaking, with tears falling down her face. I stepped over his body and pried the gun out of her hand.

"That's enough, ma. Give me the gun." I instructed, wrapping my arms around her and hugging her as tightly as I could.

"I didn't know, Keizon. Please don't hate me. I would never let him hurt you or Tasia. When I said I wanted to turn over a new leaf and be a mother, I meant it, Keizon. Lynwood was going to try to get you to tell him personal shit about Draylon. I believe he was working with the FEDs, but I don't have concrete evidence. Honestly, I went off my woman's intuition, and it's never wrong. We can't ever tell Tasia about this. Promise me what just happened will never leave this room." La-La pleaded.

"No worries. I never intended to tell her. I'll get this cleaned up. Go and take everything off and get rid of it. Pack whatever you need because you can't live here anymore. I love you, La- La."

"I love you too, son." She kissed me on the cheek and rushed out of the living room.

I looked down at my father's dead body and could not believe what the fuck had transpired. La-La had shocked the fuck out of me. I kind of wished Tasia could have seen our mother putting in work. I'm lowkey mad as fuck because I had every intention of murking him myself. There was no way I could let him live for speaking on the Prince family, anyway. It would have been bad for business all the way around. While I know I've earned their trust and loyalty. It's a lot of shit going on that got them questioning the people around them. The last thing I needed was for them to get wind of the shit Lynwood was on.

Looking down at my watch. I realized I had two hours before I needed to be at the airport. That gave me enough time to get rid of this nigga's body. I couldn't wait to see my sister. It was imperative I have a sit down with Tasia because of the way she was moving. It lets me know she forgot who the fuck I am. I don't care what the fuck she got going on with Horse. Tasia had better not ever forget I'm still her big brother. I needed my sister to know that no matter what I'll always have her back.

| | | | |

Later That Night

"Thank you, big bro. I really appreciate you and Belladonna letting me stay here," Tasia expressed.

"What the fuck are you thanking me for? It's like you forgot I'm your big brother or some shit."

"Really, Keizon?"

"Hell yeah, Tasia! I'm really feeling some type of way behind you ignoring me." I flamed up a blunt and hit it a couple of times before passing it to her.

"I'm sorry. I made you feel that way. From the bottom of my heart, that wasn't my intention. Besides being in my feelings about the things that transpired between me and Horse, I simply chose not to answer your calls or your texts. It had nothing to do with me blatantly ignoring you. It was more so to keep confusion down. I don't want to put you in my business with Horse. It puts you in an awkward place. The last thing I wanted is you and Horse beefing. It wasn't that serious, Keizon."

"It was serious. We were worried sick about you. Horse was, too. Going forward, I don't give a fuck about Horse and I getting into it when it comes down to you, so never feel like you can't come to me. Let the men worry about the beefs. Horse and I had a conversation about this. As a man, I'll never overstep my boundaries. I will never allow a nigga to overstep his boundaries when it comes to my wife. It's the respect of it all. Horse is my man hundred grand, but you're my blood sister. My loyalty to you will always trump the friendship I have with him. I love you, and I'm glad you decided to come home." I leaned over, gave Tasia a brotherly hug, and kissed her forehead.

"After Belladonna checked us. I was more than happy to get my ass back home. She called me and Kateevah some bad ass mothers, which made me feel like shit. I had no business leaving my baby. Honestly, I had no business setting that fucking fire. I could have lost it all acting on them emotions. It showed me I love that man too much, which is what makes the shit worse. I'm too far gone over Horse, Keizon. I'm positive the feelings are mutual."

"I'm team Tasia, but I can assure you that nigga Horse loves you. Please don't tell him I told you this."

"What?"

"He cried when you almost killed him. Stop laughing, Tasia. See, that's why I didn't want to tell you." Her ass was laughing hard as fuck. She doesn't take shit seriously.

"No Keizon. Tell me. Was he ugly crying?"

"Like a motherfucker!" We both were laughing now.

"Good. I was crying like a motherfucker, too," she admitted.

"No lie. I laughed at Horse's ass when he first showed up at the crib looking for you. We had to calm that nigga the fuck down. You had his nerves all rattled and shit. Once he stopped being hurt, he started being pissed. That's when we were all trying to get in contact with you."

"I can't believe Horse was crying, but that still doesn't mean the feelings are mutual."

"That doesn't mean they aren't either. Men handle shit differently. One thing for sure, two for certain, Horse is not about to be crying over no woman if he didn't love her. The way he was drunk and crying let me know he loves the fuck out of you. Plus, as long as I've known him, he's never even had a main bitch. You are the first, so his feelings for you are all new to him."

Tasia was sitting quietly, taking in everything that I said. I poured us a shot and flamed up another blunt.

"He claims to love me, yet he's around here fucking on other bitches. I find it funny how he was doing all that crying, yet in my face, he was talking about co-parenting. I don't understand that nigga, big bro."

"That's the problem. How about you try understanding him instead of fighting with him? I'm in no way condoning whatever he did. All I'm saying is go about the shit differently. Horse loves the fuck out of you and my nephew. I know you love him too. I've never seen you act this way over a nigga, either. You crazy motherfuckers are really one and the same. I love you and I'm not going to ever steer you wrong. If you love that nigga and don't want to co-parent, go and tell him that. I had a long ass day, and I'm about to lay it down."

I kissed her on the forehead and left her with her thoughts. Latasia had some decisions to make. I couldn't be the one that made them for her.

When I made it up to the bedroom, Belladonna was knocked out sleeping. My wife was by far the most beautiful creature God ever created. I'm so fucking happy she belongs to me. She was always talking about how lucky she was to have snatched up her a young nigga. Hell, my young ass was the lucky one. Having her in my life as my wife makes me want to be better and do better. I'm happy she didn't ask any questions about Lynwood or La-La. I didn't want to lie to her, and I didn't want to tell her either. What happened today is something that will be going to the grave with my mother and me. It's better this way.

As I climbed into bed with Belladonna, I buried my face into her big ass titties. It was the softest place on earth.

Chapter 14: Kateevah

I had been lying in bed for hours, looking at the ceiling. It had been about a week since I came back from Vegas. Thank God I have clients who trust my stylists in my absence. My staff is also very dependable. I don't know where I would be without them. They have been holding the salon and nail spa down. I was still on an extended vacation, so I have not been doing shit but sleeping, reading, eating, getting drunk, and getting high. It's been the same routine day in and day out. I'm ashamed to admit I didn't know when I was going to get out of this funk.

Unique hurt my feelings by saying she wanted to stay with her daddy. That's what I get, though. My momma was right. Now my baby is mad at me for leaving her. It's like I'm not catching a break. That added, not having any contact with Draylon is driving me crazy.

The sound of my doorbell ringing made me sit up. I grabbed my phone to check the cameras. It irritated me to see Annalise and Granny. *What the fuck did they want?* I let them stand outside for a good fifteen minutes before opening the door.

"What y'all doing over here?"

"Hello to you too, Kateevah!" Annalise greeted me as she pushed past me. Granny wobbled her old ass in on her walking stick.

I had a feeling these old hags were about to piss me off. They looked like they were up to no good. I wasn't in the mood to deal with anyone with the last name Prince.

"What y'all doing here?"

"We're here because you need to make up with Draylon." Granny stated as she took a seat on the sofa.

"I'm sorry you all made a blank trip, but that won't be

happening. He's the one that's mad at me. I didn't do shit but be loyal, love, and respect that man. He handled me fucked up. So, I fell completely back. As a matter of fact, we're getting a divorce." I sat on the couch and grabbed the half a blunt from the ashtray.

"Shut up Kateevah! You sound dumb as hell right now. I'm not sure if you're trying to convince us or yourself. We all know you and Draylon are not about to get no fucking divorce. However, somebody has to wave the white flag, and I feel like it should be you."

All I could do was shake my head, listening to Annalise. Leave it to a nigga's mother to tell you to be the one to give in.

"With all due respect. I shouldn't have to take one for the team. He basically walked out on me. You all should be having this conversation with him."

"Nautica stayed at the house with him last night!" Granny blurted out.

No lie. A huge lump immediately formed in my throat. "So, they're back together?"

"Oh, please. They were never together. However, if you keep leaving your husband unattended, she's going to weasel her way back into our lives. I don't want that bitch around. We want you to raise DJ as your own. Let me hit that." Annalise was in rare fucking form, asking to hit my blunt, not to mention crazy as fuck talking about me raising this boy.

"Have you been drinking, Annalise? Clearly, your ass is drunk sitting across from me saying the shit you're saying."

"We did have a couple of drinks before we left the house. Nothing major," Annalise admitted.

"I'll give you one million dollars to make things right with Draylon," Granny offered.

"Granny, you're losing your mind. I don't want your money. I love Draylon enough to make shit right on the house. The love I have for him is priceless. If I take that money, I'll be proving him right about me not being loyal to him. You all are basically trying to pay me to be with him. Doing shit like this is why he's mad at us now. You all can't keep doing shit behind his back. The secrets are taking a toll on him, and I don't want to add to the bullshit he is already going through."

"We agree with you one hundred percent. That's why we're here, Kateevah. Draylon is vulnerable right now. Nautica has made it very clear that she wants them to be a family. She even went so far as to say that she would take Unique in as her own. I know you're not going to let that happen. Listen, later tonight, we're having a party at Granny's house for DJ. You should come."

I held my breath, listening to Annalise spill those lies about Nautica, saying she would be on step mammy shit. Draylon is not crazy. He knows I'll kill him and her ass. Clearly, these two busybody-ass women came here with an agenda.

"What time does the party start, Thelma and Louise?"

"Eight o'clock. Bring Latasia, too. She and Horse need to get their shit together. It's time for this family to get back on track. See you tonight."

Annalise hugged me, and I really wanted to push her ass away. She's part of the reason we are into it. I can't fully be mad at her, though. She divulged a secret to me, and I could have told Draylon. However, I didn't, and I have to deal with the repercussions of that.

"I'm still going to put that money in your account. Think of it as reparations for your pain and suffering," Granny declared with a grin on her face.

"Your ass always giving money out. Just how much is the Prince family really worth?" I questioned her old, slick ass. She was always throwing money around like it was nothing.

"Let's just say we come from a whole lot of old money, and we are getting a whole lot of new money. You are Mrs. Draylon Prince, and you've earned every dollar thus far, not to mention the money you'll get in the future. Thank you for giving us our little Unique. See you tonight." We all exchanged hugs, and they left my house.

Minutes later, I got a message from my bank showing a million-dollar deposit. I just sat looking at all the zeros. Most women have got much less for their pain and suffering. The funny thing is, Draylon has never caused me pain or caused me to suffer.

He has shown me the purest form of love since we reunited. I couldn't ask for a better husband. Of course, the bitch Nautica wanted my life. What woman wouldn't want it? I'm not sure what Annalise and Granny are up to. All I know is they want to make it worth my while. Fuck it. I'm a million dollars richer. Let me go make shit right with my husband.

| | | | |

From the moment I arrived at the party, I had been sipping. It was the only thing I could do to calm my nerves. Draylon had yet to arrive, and I assumed the kids were with him. In the distance, I observed Nautica walking around, looking so happy. Honestly, I couldn't even be mad at her. She had been released from prison and reunited with her son. The mother in me is elated for her, while the woman in me hates her fucking guts. The bitch was bad, and she knew it. She worked the room effortlessly. I took notice of how everybody was embracing Nautica. I have to keep remembering she was actually a part of this family before I was even a thought. There were people in attendance that I didn't even know.

"That bitch thinks she's Princess Diana," Tasia sassed, bringing me out of my thoughts.

"I swear, she is acting like this is her party."

"Just say the word, and we can turn that bitch every which way but loose. You know I'm dying to tear her ass up."

Before I could respond, I observed Draylon, Unique, and his son walk through the front door. Nautica quickly rushed over to her son and wrapped her arms around him.

"He couldn't deny that boy if he wanted to," Tasia stated.

"I know, right? DJ and Unique look just like him. I'm happy he has both of his kids in his life. Being a father is something that he takes very seriously, and I love that about him."

"Have you talked to him?"

"We talk about Unique, but there hasn't been much of a conversation about us. How about you? Have you talked to Horse?"

"Nah, I've been avoiding his ass like the plague. I sent La-La to pick my baby up this morning. I honestly don't know what to say to him. I'm mad at him, and I'm mad at myself because I miss him. That Demon Dick still has a hold on me, and it makes no sense."

"It's the same way I'm feeling about Draylon. Why does that nigga got to be so fine?" I bit down on my bottom lip as I watched him work the room.

"Go say something to him, friend. One of us has to have some courage around this motherfucker. This coward shit is blowing me!"

"I have yet to meet his son formally, so I guess I'll start there."

Before heading out to introduce myself, I grabbed the gift I had gotten for DJ. My daughter noticed me and ran full speed ahead toward me.

"Hi, Mommy, come say hello to my big brother." Unique was basically pulling me toward DJ. He was standing in between Nautica and Draylon. I could tell my presence irritated her.

"This is my mommy, DJ. Look, she got you a gift." Unique was so excited. It was cute to see her happy about having a brother.

"Hi, DJ. I'm Kateevah. Nice to meet you. Here I got you something. Open it. Hopefully, your mom and dad will be okay with it."

"Wowww! A Rolex. Look, Dad, it's just like yours."

"I see! That's what's up." Draylon was smiling like a Cheshire cat, so I knew I did well with the gift.

"Look at the back. It has your name engraved on it. Let me put it on you," I offered.

Nautica quickly walked off.

"Thank you, Kateevah. Come on, Unique. Let's go show Uncle Horse."

"Okay, but don't gamble with him. If you don't have any money, he'll take your jewelry as payment. I had to give him my chain," Unique warned.

My eyes widened hearing her say that. Before I could say something to her, they took off running.

"You better get my baby chain back!" We both started laughing.

"I swear to God, I didn't know. I'll get it back. Come here. Let me talk to you for a minute." Draylon grabbed my hand and led me out of the living room.

I rolled my eyes, looking at Granny and Annalise with them goofy ass grins on their faces. With each step that we took, my heart pounded rapidly. My stress and anxiety levels were through the roof. For all I know, he was about to serve me with some damn divorce papers.

"Where the fuck is your wedding ring at?" He yanked my hand up hard as fuck, looking at my bare ring finger.

"I took it off. There was no way I was about to be wearing it, not when you said our marriage was on the shelf. That was like telling me we were over, so I took it off.   " I defended.

"Well, when we get home tonight, you put that motherfucker back on. I don't care how we fall out. We will never divorce. I never should have said that stupid shit to you. I'm sorry for overreacting. I never should have questioned your loyalty, Kateevah. Baby, you've been everything to me. Any happiness I've felt or feel has come from you and my kids. I don't ever want to lose that happy feeling. Not having you in my presence these couple of weeks showed me I can't live without you. Baby, please forgive me. I love you, Mrs. Prince."

"I love you too, Draylon." He pulled me into his embrace and kissed me passionately.

"Why are you here? This party isn't for you. It's for our son! You cannot have my life. Draylon belongs to me! I can't let you have him! Bitch, I earned his love. You got it on default. That shit is not right. Who the fuck do you think you are coming here buying my son such an expensive ass gift? You will never be his mother. That's my son!" Nautica seethed, looking like a deranged ass woman pointing a gun at us. Draylon quickly shielded me.

"Put that fucking gun down, Nautica! We can talk about this!" Draylon ordered.

"I'm not talking no more! I deserve you. You belong to me. I went to jail for you. I'm the mother of your namesake. I birthed your legacy, not her! That little girl doesn't even look like you. Please, Draylon. Tell her you have to be with me. Don't make me kill you and this bitch! If I can't have you to myself, I'll never let her have you!" Nautica threatened.

My eyes widened observing DJ casually walk into the office. When he raised the gun and shot Nautica in the back of the head, I was in such shock I was basically stuck. No words could come out of my mouth. All I could do was grip the back of Draylon's shirt.

"Noooo, sonnnnn! Why would you do that?"

"My Aunt Draya taught me that I have to protect you at all costs. She said anyone that wants you dead will eventually want me dead. Because I am the heir to the Prince's throne, it's my duty to lay down all enemies. I love you, Daddy," DJ explained.

"What the fuck?" Horse appeared in the doorway and quickly snatched the gun from DJ before ushering him out of the office and closing the door behind him.

I took a look at Nautica's brains lying beside her and almost passed out. What in the fuck did I just witness?

Chapter 15: Draylon

Thank God I'm built Ford tough. Otherwise, the shit that's been going on in my life would drive a weak nigga crazy. It had been a couple of hours since DJ killed Nautica, and I didn't know how to feel. After everything that has happened, Draya is still fucking with me from the grave. Parts of me regret killing her. I feel like there will always be unanswered questions. It's like, on one hand, she had a beef with me, and on the other, she loved her big brother. That shit got me feeling so confused. I honestly don't know if I'm coming or going, nor do I know how to feel about things. This is some shit straight out them novels Kateevah be reading.

I had been dreading having a much-needed conversation with my son. The words he spoke after pulling that trigger had me fucked up in the head. It wasn't even the words. Honestly, it was his behavior afterward. The little nigga was acting like a regular nine-year-old. Observing him had me shook. He came from my nut sack, but Draya had raised him to kill shit.

"Cut that off for a minute. We need to talk." DJ was playing the game in the room he now had at our house.

"Am I in trouble?"

"Nah, we have to talk about what you did, though. I'm not about to treat you like a little kid anymore. Today, you did some grown-man shit that, in a way, was wrong. Nautica was your mother. You do understand that she's dead. You killed her, and there is no coming back from that."

"I know. Aunt Draya taught me that death is final. Kateevah can be my mom now. Plus, I have Grandma Annalise and Granny." DJ really didn't care. I could see it in his eyes. It lowkey had me a little shook.

"Look at me. Going forward you allow me to protect you. It's not your job to protect me. Yes, you are the heir to the throne. However, in the meantime, I want you to grow up like a normal kid. Running the family business will come later when you're an adult. Where did you get that gun from, anyway?"

"Aunt Draya bought it for me. She told me to keep it in my bookbag and always keep my backpack on me."

"Well, the only thing you'll have in your backpack going forward is shit for school. I love you, son. I'm not okay with what you did today. However, I'm proud to have a son who protected me. I'll protect you forever, son. Give me a hug!"

DJ stood up and hugged me tight, and I felt his love for me in my heart.

Before walking out of the room, I looked up and saw Draya clear as day. She mouthed the words *"I love you"* and disappeared. For a minute, I was stuck in place. Once I gathered myself, I rushed out of the room. That shit had spooked the fuck out of me.

As I headed down the hall, I heard Tasia and Horse fucking in the guest bedroom. I couldn't help but stop and listen.

"Tell me you love this, Demon Dick!"

"Yes, I love that Demon Dick! I'm not going to try to kill you no more!"

"Man, keep that shit down!" I shouted, banging on the door. The door opened, and Horse was standing there naked as hell. I swear that nigga don't give a fuck.

"Sorry, bro! We are making up for lost time."

"Man, take your ass back in there!"

When I reached the bedroom, Kateevah was coming out of the bathroom. She had a towel wrapped around her. Droplets of water glistening on her breasts that sat up like pillows. It had been a minute since I had them pretty motherfuckers swinging in my face while she rode a nigga dick.

"I thought you left."

"I'm not going anywhere. Where the fuck is your ring at?" It irritated me seeing that she still hadn't put it on.

"Calm down, Draylon. I was just about to grab it from my

jewelry box."

"Are you okay?" I sat on the edge of the bed and flamed up a blunt. It felt good as hell to be home with my wife for a change.

"Yes. I'm okay. The question is, are you okay?"

"You're here with me, Kateevah, so I know I'll be okay. Right about now, I'm putting all Prince family matters in the hands of Horse for the next year. I just want to work on my family. It's you, me, Unique, and DJ now. In order for us to be a normal family, I have to be hands-on. We have to show DJ a normal life."

"You are the king of our family. We are nothing without your leadership. As much as I want to agree with you stepping down, you can't. The family you come from needs you, and the family you have created needs you. There are still threats to be handled and money to be made. I'll hold us down while you run the streets with your gangsters. A new life and chapter is on the horizon for our family. Only you have the pen that completes our story. You can't stop now, Draylon." Kateevah explained.

I observed Kateevah pull her hair up in a high ponytail before removing the towel and dropping to her knees in front of me. I stood up, and she did not hesitate to pull down my pants.

"Promise me you'll keep running shit." My eyes rolled in the back of my head as my wife started giving me the sloppiest top ever.

"I promise!" I moaned out in pleasure as I drifted off to a future time and place.

This love between gangsters and their BBWs is top-tier. That's how you know it's a love story that has the potential to stand the test of time. It's the love we share and the love we make. It's the bonds we break and the enemies we annihilate. We're the Prince family and wouldn't have it any other way.

Our story isn't finished yet. We'll see you in the next chapter of *A Gangster's BBW Obsession.*

The End For Now...

Made in the USA
Columbia, SC
08 September 2024

41986089R00070